Dying Flames

Dying Flames

ROBERT BARNARD

First published in Great Britain in 2005 by
Allison & Busby Limited
Bon Marché Centre
241-251 Ferndale Road
London SW9 8BJ
http://www.allisonandbusby.com

A catalogue record for this book is available from
the British Library.

10 9 8 7 6 5 4 3 2 1

ISBN 0 7490 8236 4

Printed and bound in Wales by
Creative Print and Design, Ebbw Vale

ROBERT BARNARD was born in Essex. He was educated at Balliol College, Oxford, and after completing his degree he taught English at universities in Australia and Norway, where he completed his doctorate on Dickens. He returned to England to become a full-time writer and currently lives with his wife in Leeds, Yorkshire. The couple are currently collaborating on a Brontë encyclopaedia. In his spare time he enjoys opera, crosswords and walking the dog. In 2003 Robert Barnard was the recipient of the prestigious CWA Cartier Diamond Dagger, an award in recognition of a lifetime's achievement in crime writing.

Novels by Robert Barnard

Death of an Old Goat
A Little Local Murder
Death on the High C's
Blood Brotherhood
Unruly Son
Posthumous Papers
Death in a Cold Climate
Mother's Boys
Sheer Torture
Death and the Princess
The Missing Brontë
Little Victims
Corpse in a Gilded Cage
Out of the Blackout
Disposal of the Living
Political Suicide
Bodies
Death in Purple Prose
The Skeleton in the Grass
At Death's Door
Death and the Chaste Apprentice
A City of Strangers

1

The Girl and the Boys

When he heard the knock on his hotel room door, Graham Broadbent thought it must be the maid with the extra pillow that he'd phoned to ask the housekeeper for. But when he opened the door it was a fair-headed girl with a low-cut top that emphasized her breasts. Graham always noticed breasts.

"Yes?" he said.

"Hello, Dad," said the girl.

Graham looked, and swallowed.

"I beg your pardon?"

The girl let out a sort of delighted chuckle.

"I recognised you at once from the photograph on the dust-jackets of your books. We have a lot of them at home, and Mum always gets the new ones from the library. They know her there, and keep them for her automatically. She always describes you to them as 'an old friend'."

Graham put on a cold, distant voice.

"I'm afraid you're under a misapprehension. I don't have a teenage daughter."

"I'm nineteen going on twenty, but I've always looked younger than my age. Can I come in?"

Graham thought quickly. The girl had presumably no plans to seduce him or get herself seduced: if she had, she'd chosen a highly original chat-up line. Still, a mere look could have told any middle-aged man she spelt danger. He had felt stirrings of danger already.

"Why don't we go down to the bar and have a coffee instead?" he suggested.

The girl shrugged but looked cunning.

"Well, if you don't mind having your private life talked about around Colchester," she said.

Graham only paused for a second, then stood aside. The girl breezed into the room and looked around.

"Nice!" she said. "I've only ever stayed in B&Bs, but I can tell this is a good hotel."

"And you live – where?"

"Romford. Quite a nice little semi-detached. Mum gets money from my stepfather for both of us children. He'd adopted me, you see. And I've got a younger brother – Adam."

"So she's been married –?"

She shrugged again, this time a wry expression on her face.

"Oh yes, she was for a while. But she's very independent now."

On the basis of the alimony, Graham thought.

"You say you're nearly twenty," he said. "So that means you were born in the second half of 1984."

"August the twenty-first."

"So you were conceived —"

"It's not a dirty word."

"I paused because I was doing my maths. Conceived around early November 1983."

She grimaced.

"If you say so. Mum's never said I was premature or overdue."

"Even if you were, I was in Mali from April 1983 to mid-January the next year."

"So?"

"Has your mother ever talked about being in Mali?"

"No…But I know she's had a holiday in Tunisia."

"I've never been there in my life."

The girl was sitting on the sofa now, and stretching her long legs. She looked very fetching, Graham thought. The stirrings came back, unmistakable this time.

"How do I know where she went or where you've been? I wasn't born. All I know is what you *did*."

"You only know that by hearsay," said Graham, asperity taking over from lust. "Let me tell you I was extremely careful about what I *did*, as you call it. I was working for Christian Aid."

"What does that mean? That you only fucked black women, where there'd be no repercussions? That was pretty cowardly, wasn't it? But you must have made exceptions."

"This conversation is becoming ridiculous: I think you should leave. I have a dinner to go to tonight."

"I know. School reunion or something. But I won't leave." Her face began to crumple up, Graham couldn't decide whether from emotion or from art. "You don't seem to realize how disappointing this is. I'd hoped for so much. I'm your *daughter*! I thought you might be pleased."

"If you expected a fatted calf you've been living in Cloud Cuckoo Land."

"I don't know what I expected but it wasn't to be rejected like this." Her shoulders began to heave.

Graham felt helpless. He was quite unable to decide how much of the girl's crushing disappointment was in fact an act preparatory to blackmail. She might not be aware she had nothing to blackmail him with.

"So be it," he said. "I'm a horrible man. But you have the consolation of knowing that the horrible man you're talking to is not your father."

"Oh no I don't. Mum has told me ever since I was little who my father was. She told me then that my father had written books – or it may have been just one book then. We followed your career until you became quite famous. I've always known that one day I would meet you."

"Well, you seem to have made damned sure you did!" Graham exploded. Then he regained his apparent calm. "Try to understand, nothing you've said leads me to believe I've met your mother."

He had gone too far, and the girl knew it.

"How do you know that? You haven't even asked our names!"

"Well, I —"

"I'll tell you anyway. My mum's called Margaret Webster, and I'm Christabel. People call me Christa."

"I've never heard of either of you."

"She's from Colchester too. She was at the Girls' High School while you were at the Grammar School. She's a year younger than you."

"So she says. There were a lot of girls at the Girls' High I never knew. I've never heard of her."

"She was Margaret Somers. That was her maiden name. Everyone calls her Peggy."

Graham turned quickly to the dressing table, picked up a tie, and began putting it on.

"I haven't got much time. I'm guest of honour at this dinner…"

"Oh, I know. Gran always sends us the *Essex Weekly*. It said the guest of honour was some eighty-year-old teacher, poor old git, and that you were *special* guest."

"Whatever," said Graham, combing his hair.

"I love this," said the girl called Christa.

"Love what?"

"Seeing you do all these personal, intimate little things."

"Is combing my hair intimate?"

"Yeah – in a way. It's the sort of thing I'd have seen my dad do if you'd been around to *be* my dad."

"I get your drift."

"It was never quite like that with my stepfather. He was always just my mother's bloke."

"I can imagine. Now, if you'll come along —"

"Oh, all right. I wouldn't want to keep you from your eighty-year-old teacher! I'm going to see my gran in Stanway anyway."

He ushered her out into the corridor and firmly locked the door. Then they went downstairs and through the public rooms, Christa all the time talking about her gran and the cats she kept, Graham glad to keep her on those topics to prevent her getting on to others closer to home. When they got out into the High Street there was a taxi a few yards up the street, and Graham hailed it. As it drew up to the kerb he turned to the girl.

"Well, I'll say goodbye. Remember I have no idea why your mother has put this notion into your head, but there is nothing in it, no question of my being your father. No question at all."

He got into the taxi, but the girl held the door open as he belted himself in.

"But you recognised the name Peggy Somers, didn't you?" she shouted above the traffic's roar. Then she slammed the door shut, waved, smiled, and made her way up the High Street in the other direction.

As the taxi made its tortuous way to the White Bull Hotel in Lexden, Graham sat slumped in meditation. She was a fetching creature, this Christa. If she had done anything but claim to be his daughter he would have been titillated by her frank approach. Even as it was he was…interested. But the claim to be his daughter definitely damped down his habitual sexual curiosity. After all, ages were notoriously difficult to guess. It was always a little disillusioning to find that a soap's naive little twelve-year-old was really played by a budding actress of eighteen. This tantalising intrusion into his life who claimed to be nineteen could easily turn out to be twenty-six. And even if she was the age she claimed, there had been occasions in Mali, not many but one or two, when the strict boundaries that, in deference to his employers, he had constricted himself within, had been…leapt over.

And then there was the matter of Peggy Somers. But that was quite another thing, and the connection of that event in his life with the visit he had just had was something Graham felt quite unable to fathom.

When he arrived at the White Bull he found that the reunion was taking on a form familiar to him from his two previous attendances. Faces familiar but older, more tired, came up and greeted him, and his brain tried, usually without avail, to fix names to them. Faces almost unchanged by time also came up, arousing jealousy and irritation in equal measure in Graham's brain, and a similar inability to dredge up names. "Good to see you," he said to most of them, and it was almost true. This going back presented, encapsulated, a summary of what time could do, and what it sometimes refrained from doing. In his case, he was well aware, time had left its usual Satanic footprints: on his face in the form of lines, subtle collapses; less visibly its effects showed themselves in a loss of zest, of the energy of youth. He felt himself lacking now in any sense of adventure, of any love of life. He was, like these other men of his age, stuck. Stuck in a quite large hole, but stuck nevertheless.

"Is your wife with you?" asked Roderic Sprott, one of his

classmates back in the nineteen-seventies. The question, since this was an all-male gathering, could only mean, "has she come with you to sample the delights of Colchester?"

"No," said Graham. "We've...split up."

"Oh, I'm awfully sorry. I didn't —" began Sprott, but Graham gave a wave of the hand and turned away to look at the crowd around the hotel's bar, where George Long, as gregarious at eighty as he had been at fifty, was in the centre of an admiring group. During Graham's schooldays his voice – not sergeant-majorish, but scything through the air like a mighty scimitar – had dominated games afternoons, with exhortations, comments congratulatory or cutting, and tips which those more sporty than Graham had valued. In classrooms George Long had read Chaucer as to the medieval manner born, and had brought Shakespeare vividly to life. His school plays had marked many boys (and the odd pupil from the Girls' High School) for life: indeed some said their lives had been anti-climactic after the highpoints of playing Macbeth, Hamlet or John Tanner. Just listening to the voice, seeing the face with its HG Wells moustache, made Graham feel he was back in 4C (C for Classics, the highest form; S for Science had been counted as definitely second-rate). It was disconcerting to be once again the timid, humourless boy who lived in the shadows. The child is not father to the man, he thought.

A gong sounded, and the habitués trooped obediently up the stairs to the dining room. Graham let them go, finishing his gin and tonic so as to be ready for the always abundant wine at the table. He was listening, or just nodding at, a man called Ted Bareacres who was telling him about the finer points of his Richard the Second. When they made their way up the stairs they found that the only places available were at a table dominated by the burly figure of Garry McCartney. He was standing up and waving at the latecomers.

"Plenty of room here," he called out. Graham's heart sank. At both his previous attendances at the celebrations of George Long's great age, he had been favoured with accounts of how Garry had scored the deciding try in the last minutes of Colchester Grammar's historic win at rugby over the boys of Chelmsford High. As he took his place, Roderic Sprott beside him, Graham would have liked to say "I hope we're not going to talk rugger," but he thought after a look at McCartney's bulk, that he wouldn't after all. He had always fought shy of the sporty crowd when he was at school.

The food at the White Bull was excellent, as always: that's why it was chosen, along with its proximity to the Grammar School, which made it convenient for such Old Boys as wanted to make a sentimental pilgrimage of return. It was towards the end of the main course (duck or halibut, with a vegetarian option that looked like dog's vomit – no care was taken of the option, because red-blooded males from the Royal Grammar School shouldn't want vegetarian options) that Graham heard Garry McCartney from the other end of the table. He was well-launched into the story of his triumphant intervention in the historic match against Chelmsford.

"I got the ball from old Digger – remember Digger? One of the best – and I was about fifteen yards in from touch on our right. But coming straight at me was this massive lock forward from Chelmsford – Christ, was he huge! Well, I dummied to go inside him, intending to take him on the outside and go for the corner, but I realised he hadn't bought the dummy, and was moving to his left and would have buried me. So, quick as a flash, I changed my mind and kept running inside, wrongfooting the bastard completely. I wrongfooted their scrumhalf as well – he was cornerflagging – and I went past him too on the inside, straight to the posts…"

And so on. Graham had heard it all before. It was like a record. Graham knew a man who had tapes of all Brian Johnston's major Test Match commentaries. It seemed to him that softening of the brain could not be more vividly demonstrated. He turned to the men around him.

"Any of you remember my hat-trick against Rumbleborough High in the summer of 'seventy-seven?" he demanded. There were sniggers. Enough of them remembered Graham's total lack of skill at any team sport or any branch of athletics to ensure that his intention was appreciated.

"That was school cricket at its finest," said Roderic Sprott.

"It would have graced a Test against Australia," said Graham with conviction. "All the main batsmen were out, but their middle men were putting up a tremendous fight. Then I was called on to bowl by Smithson – remember old Smithson? Total prat in every possible way, but he made an inspired decision there. It was precisely my double spin that was required. Well, the fifth man was despatched in a couple of balls…"

There was movement down the table. McCartney, in full reminisce, had caught wind of what was being said at the other end. He suspected someone of taking the piss. McCartney didn't mind taking the piss, but he did object to its being taken from him.

"What — ?" he began, his voice raised.

"Gentlemen and others," came the well-remembered voice from a table in the centre of the dining room. George Long, with his school-master's antennæ for trouble still alert when he was in his eighties, had known something was brewing on Table Five. Garry McCartney had frequently spelt trouble, on or off various sporting pitches, back in the nineteen-seventies, and George strongly suspected that by now he had a record with the police. He smoothly switched on the spontaneous words of welcome that he had rehearsed into his bedroom mirror that morning.

"I'm not going to go on. Well, I am, but not on *and* on. It's a great joy to me that you still want to come to my little birthday dinner, even though my seventy-fifth was several years ago now, and still a few years to go before I get the telegram from the Queen, if she's still around when I'm 100, which I'm greatly looking forward to."

Cheers rose, as he had known they would, from around all the tables.

"You won't be surprised if I say that it's particularly warming that so many people here remember the plays, whether they had big parts in them or not. We have a Hamlet here today, a Richard the Second. But we also have some who have graced smaller roles. Many of you will remember *St Joan* for the lovely girl who played Joan herself..." He seemed to falter momentarily, perhaps because he couldn't remember her name. "But today we have with us the man who played the Steward in the first scene. Not a part that gets you straight into drama school, so he went to university instead. He also, fortunately for us, went into the school of life as well. I've never been quite sure how you can *avoid* going to the school of life, by the bye," (cue for laughter) "and, he made such good use of his knowledge and experience there that he's become a very considerable novelist, with two Booker Prize nominations to his credit. You all know who I mean – Graham Broadbent, our Special Guest."

The applause was warm, though not particularly involved. Graham was a credit to the school rather than someone they remembered at all well. George went on to a further five minutes of reminiscence and thanks to all those who had arranged the dinner, and then sat down with impeccable timing. But not without a nervous glance at Table Five, which was applauding enthusiastically with the rest. Satisfied all was well, George Long turned to the Old Boys around him.

But all was not restored to good humour at Graham's table, and he was a bit bemused as to the reason. Garry McCartney, after the clapping and cheers, sat slumped in his chair. Surely he was not still resenting the parody of his stupefying sporting stories? Well yes, he probably was, Graham thought. But five minutes later Garry broke into speech with Ted Bareacres, the man sitting beside him.

"Peggy," he said.

"Come again?"

"I've been trying to think of the name of the girl who played St Joan. Lovely little creature, and brilliant with it. You know me, Ted: lit-er-a-chewer is not really my thing, but she was fabulous. I was Robert de Baudricourt, and I just worshipped her. Peggy was her name."

"She was good, wasn't she? I wasn't in it, but I saw her."

"Fabulous…Peggy something…Just brilliant, she was. And then – nothing."

"What do you mean?"

"I mean what I said: nothing. Moved away quickly. Nobody knew where she'd gone – not her schoolmates, not George."

"I expect the parents moved."

"I expect they did. But why, and why were there no contacts kept up? There were rumours. I bet someone knows."

"Who knows? Knows what?"

"There were rumours about him too. More than one rumour. But if I get to know who the guttersnipe was —" Was it just Graham's self-consciousness that said that McCartney was not just looking across the table but was looking at him? "If I knew who the guttersnipe was I'd make him *pay*."

Bareacres was looking at him, mystified.

"Why should you care? That's the drink talking."

"Everyone who knew her cared. She was like a…a shining light…I wish I could remember her name."

People around Garry McCartney were grinning at his violence in the cause of a girl whose name he could barely remember. But Graham wasn't grinning. Graham could remember the name of the girl who had played St Joan. And he was thinking that this might be the last year he came to the reunion for George Long.

2

The Loneliness of the Long-Distance Author

The next morning Graham was disturbed in his hotel room by a ringing telephone. Plenty of people knew he was staying at the King William in Colchester, but none that he could think of would want to ring him at seven forty-five.

"Graham Broadbent," he said.

"Oh, I say, look, I mean – this is Garry McCartney. The chap who —"

"I remember which chap you are, Garry," said Graham coolly. "What can I do for you?"

"Well, it's just that…well, people said – Ted Bareacres rang last night, and he said people were saying – well, that I'd come on a bit strong yesterday at the reunion."

"A bit strong, Garry?" said Graham smoothly. "I don't see that. You felt strongly so you spoke strongly. Nothing wrong in that."

"Good of you…er, Graham. I do feel strongly. People think I'm a bit of a thug, but really I'm very sensitive. And she was so —"

"She was lovely. I didn't know you and she had anything going, but I just had a bit part with you in the first scene."

"We *didn't* have anything going." The voice was suddenly loud, then softened again. "I told you, I'm the sensitive type. I was seventeen, but I wasn't…you know, experienced. And in those days kids weren't at it at twelve, like they are today. I worshipped her from afar – that's how you literary types would put it, isn't it? I could see she was something different, way out of my league. And then when some oaf went and got her in the family way, or that was what the rumour said…well, I just went ballistic."

"You didn't think, Garry, did you, that it was me who did it?"

"No. You know how it is, old man. You get funny ideas after you've had two or three drinks."

"Because apart from backstage, when everyone was watching, the only time I met her was one day when I went to see that old Anglo-Saxon church, near —"

"You don't have to explain, old man. I just got this mad idea into my head. Will you just forget about it? *Please*?"

"Of course, Garry. I've forgotten about it already. We neither of us had much to do after the first scene, did we? Just be extras and shout 'rhubarb'. But it was a joy just watching her, I agree with you there. Happy times. Well, I'm off to my breakfast."

"Oh, of course. Hope I haven't kept you. Have the Full English, eh? Only way to justify the prices these hotels charge."

For some reason when Graham went down to the Breakfast Room he didn't fancy one of the monstrous fry-ups that hotels specialise in. He had a couple of poached eggs and bacon, then filled up on toast and marmalade and coffee. He settled up his bill, keeping the receipts for the Inland Revenue, who subsidised quite a few of Graham's pleasures, then finished packing and took the case out to his car.

He was very thoughtful during the hour-long drive home to Suffolk. He had half expected the girl to reappear at his door after breakfast, and felt disappointment in the pit of his stomach that she hadn't. What was her name? Christa, that was it. It sounded somehow German, or perhaps Scandinavian, but she said it was just short for Christabel. He fantasised that she might have hidden herself on the floor at the back of the car, and even, on a stretch of deserted road, turned round and had a look.

"Silly fool," he said to himself. Being a realist he added: "She wasn't even small."

He got home to Hepton Magna by half-past eleven. It was not one of those ostentatiously villagey villages, just a moderately attractive collection of small and middle-sized houses and cottages, solid and unshowy. A bit like Graham Broadbent novels one interviewer had said, but she had specialised in the casual sneer. Graham's was one of the middle-sized houses, now rather too big since his wife had decamped. While the toasted cheese for his lunch was under the grill he walked around the ground floor and noted for the umpteenth time how little of his wife, who had been gone for nearly a year, was now left in the house. It was not that she had lacked personality, or that he had tried systematically to erase all trace of her, merely that she had not cared to impress herself on the house. Probably she had guessed from early on that the marriage was unlikely to be a long-lasting one. Graham was a one-night-stand lover – two or three nights at a pinch. He gave little and he took little. It did not make for a stable marriage, and Ellen had slipped out of his life with as little fuss as he had made about having her in it.

"At least you'll be free now," she had said on the phone. "You can do what you want when you want. No more subterfuges."

Sitting with his sizzling plate at the small table in the dining room Graham felt a certain satisfaction at being home. Around him were the tools of his trade – the reference books, the classic novels he loved, the works of his contemporaries. And there was the modest achievement of the shelf-full of his own novels – those low-keyed stories of lonely people that one sarky critic had described as "like Anita Brookner without the passion." Graham did not apologise for his books. They were like himself. They were a faithful mirror of what he was – no; of what he *had become*. Low-key, unassertive, but full of unrecognised passions.

There was no getting any writing done that day. He played some music on the CD, went to stock up on basics at the local shop, vacuumed the downstairs rooms. His mind was buzzing as he did all these things. There was every reason to do nothing about the strange incursion into his life that had occurred at Colchester. Every reason – and yet all sorts of irrational urges acted against those reasons. Graham was not a man for irrational urges. He knew that common prudence demanded that he listen to the sensible advice of his brain, and yet...

He dialled Directory Enquiries.

"What name is it, please?" the voice said.

"The name is Webster. Margaret Theresa Webster."

"And what town?"

"The town is Romford, in Essex."

"I see...Do you have an address?"

"No, I don't."

"There are two MT Websters in the Romford Directory. Oh...one is a Reverend. Could be a woman, but...Shall I give you the other number to start with?"

"Please. And could I have the address too, please?"

"I'm afraid we're not allowed to divulge addresses."

"But it will be in the Directory."

"As I say, we are not —"

"All right: the number."

The human voice was succeeded by a disembodied one.

"The number you require is 01705 642971."

The disembodied voice then offered him (probably

mendaciously) further help if he needed it, and he rang off.

Graham's first thought was to ring his editor at Harcourt and Gormsley to see if he had a South-East London telephone directory there. The thought of explaining himself put him off the idea. His editor was the first resort for any problem great and small in his professional life. The tiny bit left that was his private life he had always kept to himself. It was by now three o'clock. He decided to get into his car again and drive to Ipswich, and to its public library.

There – as so often in libraries, particularly reference libraries – the problem solved itself. In the residential directory for South East London he found:

"Webster, MT, 25 Milton Terrace, Romford 01705 642971."

He also, since he was there, noted the address of the Reverend gentleman or lady. Presumably it was not necessary: surely Christa would have told him if her mother was a minister of religion?

He pondered this last thought, though. Christa was, in his judgment, a tease. It was one of the things he found delightful about her. She had told him what it suited her to tell him at that point in their relationship. And no more. Even the "Theresa" he had had to remember for himself. She had told him nothing about her own life – whether she was employed, unemployed, a student, in a relationship, still living at home, straight, gay – nothing. He felt sure it was her intention to pursue the matter. Pursue *him*. She could even find his address without too much trouble: it appeared in an American directory of contemporary novelists, and now for the first time (because fans had not come in droves to bang on his door) he regretted giving them permission.

Or did he regret it?

He found that in the car on the way home he was weighing up in his mind the best time to drive to Romford. If he was to drive around the streets hoping for a glimpse of Christa or her mother (but would he recognise her?), when would be the best time of day to do it?

He was conscious that there was no conditional tense in his deliberations: not "should he decide to go", but a mental stance of "granted that he had decided to go." His caution, his rationality, had been thrown to the winds. His urge had taken him over. He regretted his caution and rationality, but felt excitement at their overthrow. It occurred to him that they, and indeed the whole shape of his personality, were a consequence of what had happened in the summer of the year 1979. The summer following the school production of *St Joan*.

By the time he arrived back in Hepton Magna he had decided that the early morning was the best time to visit Romford. And that it had better be done while the determination was in him. He watched the headlines on the ten o'clock news, then turned in for an early night, setting the Teasmaid for six a.m.

Driving through the streets of Romford was not a spirit-elevating experience. He had found Milton Terrace from a *London A to Z* he had bought when writing his novel *The New Prufrock* (long-listed but not short-listed for the Booker Prize in 1997). He made the street his centre of operations, and drove around noting shopping streets and office blocks where Christa might be employed and places of education where she might study. Milton Terrace itself was a street of "nice little semi-detacheds", exactly as the girl had said (Graham clocked it up as the first verified truth he had heard from her lips). It was surrounded by many others, some slightly better, some slightly worse. In the property market of his youth the differences would have meant a thousand or two either way on the market price. In today's mad world of London's and near-London's house prices the difference was probably near fifty thousand either way.

Graham groaned at the modern world. He knew about it, but did not understand it. His books more and more were getting set in the recent past. By the time he died he'd be writing historicals.

Then he saw her.

She was five minutes away from her home, in a little group with three other girls. They were talking and laughing, and now and then exchanging greetings or badinage with some boy or other. Young men, he should say. They were part of a larger group, almost all young people, and he felt sure they were all on their way to the Jeremy Bentham College, which he had noted on his drive around. He could not go as slowly as they were walking so he drew into the side of the road. As they went beyond his field of vision he drove forward again, and was just in time to see the little group turning in through the college gates and towards the main building.

He drew into the side of the road again. What did he do now? The obvious thing was to return to Milton Terrace, since Christa's mother was quite probably there on her own now. His mind rejected this at once. He was not ready to see Peggy Somers again yet. Some day he would – he was sure the time would come, and perhaps soon. But today it was all too new, too strange. He drove forward as if in a trance, then through the college gates, parking in one of the spaces reserved for visitors. Then he sat and watched the waves of young people – he felt he had never seen so many young people together at one time – until the waves ebbed to a trickle. Classes must have begun.

At twenty past nine he got out of the car and strode towards Reception. It was all rather like a hotel, he decided. Should he ask to see the Manager? The woman in Reception added to this illusion: he could imagine her behind the desk in some old-fashioned West Country hotel.

"I wonder if you could help me," he began. "My name is Graham Broadbent." There was a tiny flicker on her polite features. "I need to see the – what is it? – Principal of the College?"

"The Director."

"Ah yes. Er, I'm a stranger in Romford, and I don't have an appointment —"

"The Director is free until nine forty-five. Could I ask what you wish to see him *about*?"

"It's rather personal. I'm a writer —"

"Yes. *The Day Wanes*."

He felt absurdly pleased.

"You make things much easier. The matter is entirely personal, but it does concern someone who I think is a student at this college."

The woman opened her mouth, and Graham was sure she wanted to ask whether it was a male or female student. She was too wise to do that, asked him instead to wait for a moment, then disappeared along a corridor. When she came back she simply said "Dr Warhope will see you now," and ushered him to the Director's door.

"Ah, Mr Broadbent," said a bearded, bespectacled man, strong on authority and decisiveness. "I know *of* your books, I'm afraid, rather than knowing them as I should, but I'm afraid I'm a scientist by training. Anyway, we're honoured by your visit. And a bit curious too. Please sit down and tell me how we can help you."

Graham sat cautiously on the seat facing the director, feeling glad he was beyond being a student.

"Yes, I'll try to do that," he said. "I'd better tell you what happened to me on Tuesday. I presume anything I tell you will be in total confidence?"

"Of course." The fingers of his hands made a neat triangle on the desk.

"On Tuesday evening I was in the King William Hotel in Colchester. It is my home town, and I was there for a school reunion. There was a knock on the door, and when I opened it a girl stood outside. She was a complete stranger to me. The first thing she said was 'Hello, Dad'."

The man's eyes widened.

"I can see you must have been disturbed."

"To put it mildly. In subsequent conversation —"

"You asked her into your room?"

"Yes. I suggested coffee downstairs, but she said wasn't it too public for the conversation we were going to have? I didn't think I had any choice. In that conversation it emerged that she must have been conceived in nineteen eighty three, when I was working for Christian Aid in Mali."

"I see...Do you mind giving me her name?"

"The surname she uses I can't be sure about. Probably Webster. The Christian name is Christa. She said it was short for Christabel."

"You can never be sure these days. I do seem to remember..." He pressed keys on his computer, then looked intently at the screen. "Yes, we have a Christa Webster. Second year, has been studying Art History. It became popular when Prince William did it at St Andrews. Quite a lot of drop-outs recently...Her birth date is given as August 21st nineteen eighty-four."

"That's what she told me."

"And that makes any involvement of yourself unlikely?"

"Inconceivable…Sorry. Couldn't have chosen a worse word."

They laughed men-together laughs.

"Well really, all the information I can give you, you have," said the Director. "So far as we here can tell, she is who she says she is, and was born when she says she was born. What does the mother say?"

Graham shifted uneasily in his chair.

"She hasn't said anything to me. I haven't contacted her."

"I see. That seems to be the next step then, doesn't it?"

"Yes…I'm reluctant to do that."

He felt himself being looked at hard.

"You knew a woman called Webster in the past?"

"Somers. The girl said that was her mother's maiden name. But that was much further in the past."

"You didn't meet up with her in Mali?"

"Certainly not. But the fact that I did once know someone who may be her mother makes me reluctant to contact her. I'm afraid of involving myself in something that really has nothing to do with me."

"I can see that. Well, it would be impertinent for me to advise you what to do. Me a micro-biologist, you a novelist with a grasp of motives and character. And you now have all the information that we have here."

"Yes, and I'm grateful for that," said Graham, standing up. "And grateful to you for your time."

"Oh, don't mention it. It has provided a much-needed change from adolescent angst. Though perhaps if I knew all the facts, it wouldn't seem so much of a change, eh?"

Graham was aware that his face gave him away, and he

merely murmured: "Maybe not."

"I said I wasn't going to advise you, but the habit is ingrained, with a job like mine. Shouldn't you make a decision: either get to the bottom of this, or get out of it as quickly and completely as possible?"

Graham kept his face as blank as possible, and said:

"Thank you again."

But in his heart he was wondering if Christa would allow him to get out of this quickly and completely. He rather thought that Dr Warhope's choice was no choice at all.

3

Peggy

Graham dithered sadly before fixing on a date for a return to Romford. It wasn't as though he was in the middle of a book. The next novel was mulching away in his mind, at the stage where all the crucial events and characters were open to question and revision. Truth to tell, the book was contending with real life: nothing that had happened in Colchester or since could be incorporated into *Events and Their Shadows* (provisional title) so in a sense it was either/or: life or novel. Graham told himself it would be a disaster (artistic and possibly legal) to build a novel on recently experienced events and emotions. And yet – how he was tempted to do just that!

In the end he made a decision about Romford. He remembered Lucetta and Elizabeth in *The Mayor of Casterbridge* agreeing to meet to discuss an important matter "the first fine day next week." How sensible! How right for the English climate, which most years offers few and isolated fine days – days that should be chosen to do anything interesting in. Hardy was always good on weather. He would go to Romford on the first fine day of next week.

Thursday was fine. It was fine when he got up, and it had been predicted as fine the night before. There was no getting away from it. There was excitement in him, but it contended with fear of disappointment. Nothing was ever uncomplicated and "straight on" with Graham. Meeting up with an old girlfriend was a sort of emotional minefield. The possibilities for disillusion were limitless. Then another thought struck him: had Peggy even been a "girlfriend", in the usual meaning of the term?

The feeling of unease in the pit of his belly increased as, over a breakfast of toast, he faced up to the fact that he had formulated no plan. He had no idea of how he was going to confront her, or with what. *Was* he going to confront her at all? Couldn't it just be fabricated to seem like a fortuitous meeting, during which they could talk about this and that, mostly things in the past that were innocuous?

Yet he had the materials for a confrontation, that was for sure. She had furnished her daughter with a false paternity, and he was the victim of her deception. One of the heroes of his novels would have had a clear idea of how he would conduct himself and what he wanted to get out of the interview, even if he ended the encounter more doubtful and less fired-up than he went into it. Graham on the other hand was quite unsure of his tactics, and had to content himself with the feeble resolution that he would "see how things turned out." It occurred to him as he drove across the boundary of Romford that this could be a recipe for disaster.

He found Milton Terrace again without much difficulty and parked the car outside number twenty-five. There were no lights on in the house, but why should there be on a fine September morning at ten-thirty? He let himself through the front gate and walked up the path, noting the dead roses that lined its once-neat beds. He rang the front door bell, and stood listening to the silence. Of course Peggy could still be in bed. He rang again.

"Are you looking for Mrs Webster?"

It was the next-door house to his right, where an elderly woman was coming out of her front door with a shopping trolley.

"That's right."

"She works at Halliburton's mornings – has done for years.

Are you a friend?"

"In a way. Let's say a one-time friend."

"Only you don't look like the usual…" Her voice faded away. "I just thought I shouldn't have said anything about her if you were sort-of official. Like a debt collector or something. But if you really are a friend."

"I am. From years ago in Colchester."

"Oh, Colchester! That's a *nice* town. I wouldn't have moved here from there, not for the world. But still, they say she had no choice, or her parents didn't. Anyway, you'll find her in Halliburton's."

"And Halliburton's is — ?"

"The greengrocer's in Wayland Road." She waved a hand to her right. "Only greengrocer's we've got left around here. Nowadays it's all supermarkets, isn't it? Still, their fruit and veg section always looks lovely and clean, doesn't it? Some people don't like a lot of dirt with their potatoes and carrots."

And she nodded to him and went off to the left.

Graham got into his car and headed in the direction she had indicated. Two minutes later he saw the sign Wayland Road, and drove off into a quiet side-street to park.

Wayland Road was a street of shops – not large High Street ones, but fairly busy ones serving that part of Romford. The shopkeepers looked as if they were suffering from shopping precincts and from supermarkets where the vegetables didn't look as if they'd come out of the earth, but were still putting up a brave fight against the modern world. Graham stood on the corner, casting his eyes up and down the shops on the other side of the street. There it was: Halliburton's Greengrocery and General Store, painted but fading on a board across the door and windows, with a blackboard advertising prices and special bargains standing on the pavement. He dallied his way in its direction, then stood outside the window as if he was fascinated by the displays of carrots and courgettes, along with special Indian and Caribbean delicacies.

Inside the shop, beside and hovering near the till, were a thin bespectacled couple, who looked more like university lecturers than greengrocers. Probably militant vegetarians, Graham thought, because he had a set of prejudices which he cherished. Serving a customer was a stoutish, fleshy woman with fluttering hands. He edged closer to the door.

"That's a little over a pound, Mrs Jackson – is that all right? And then it was a cabbage, wasn't it? This looks a nice one, doesn't it? Fifty-five p that one is…"

He still hadn't seen her face, but his heart seemed to have stopped. That was the voice. The one he had listened to off-stage, the one with the assumed rural accent, the one that cleaved through the Colchester Grammar School hall (he had listened at the back as well) – the voice that had touched every heart. And in particular every male heart.

"Is that all for today? That's fine. Oh, hello Mrs Woodcruft. What is it for you, then?"

That was the voice that had promised "to crown the Dauphin in Rheims Cathedral…And to make the English leave France." And when Robert de Baudricourt (that had been Garry McCartney) had sarcastically said "Anything else?" she had replied with a sweetness that had set his heart jumping in his throat: "Not just at present, thank you, Squire."

And this was the voice that was now selling cabbages and turnips.

She turned in his direction, without seeing him. The face was plumper, older of course, but still wonderfully attractive. If the neighbour had been implying a succession of male visitors to her house (*had* she been? Graham's brain throbbed at the thought, as it had not when she said it) it was not surprising. Graham swallowed hard and pushed open the door of the shop.

Peggy was just finishing serving Mrs Woodcruft and ushering her in the direction of the cash desk. She turned towards Graham, and her mouth opened to ask what she could get him. But she paused for a second, and then said:

"It's Graham, isn't it? Graham Broadbent? This is a nice surprise. I always knew you'd turn up some day."

She spoke as if it was a delightful coincidence, but also, oddly, as if it had been bound to happen. Graham rather resented the idea that he was bound to turn up in the course of time in a back street of Romford. The President of the Immortals had no such plan for him, and she must surely have realized that she was the only reason for his appearance in Halliburton's Greengrocery and General Store.

"Hello Peggy," he said, trying to make his voice sound assured and relaxed. "It's been a long time."

"Yes, time hasn't stood still for either of us," she said, but with a coquettish tipping of the head as if willing him to say that it had for her. But Graham's moment of heart-stop was over, and he was in no mood to be coquetted by an old flame.

"No, we can't buck the universal trend," he said firmly.

"Look, I have my coffee break in ten minutes' time," said Peggy. "We could go to Genevieve's down the road. The coffee's all right, and the cakes are lovely."

"Take your break now, Peggy," said the woman at the cash-desk. "We're not busy, so you can take your time."

They know who I am, thought Graham. And they know the connection between us. Or the supposed connection.

"That would be nice," he said. "There's a lot of catching-up to be done in a short time."

Her face briefly registered disappointment at this, but she went into the back of the shop. Graham saw her reflected in the glass of the door taking off her overall, then touching up her light make-up in a mirror on the wall. It took hardly any time, and no one would begrudge a woman in her forties a few moments to put her face in order, yet Graham felt in his stomach the feeling of a big hand gripping him.

Then she came out, and they walked past nine or ten business premises, then into Genevieve's Coffee Bar, all potted plants and amarylli. They paused at the counter, where icy cakes, buns and scones were displayed. Peggy's eyes lit up with what must be greed or sugar deficiency.

"I'm going to have…the Viennese Whirl. Don't they look lovely? Oh, and look at those! They're new…But I mustn't be greedy."

"No, do have one. Two – what? – cappuccinos, a Viennese Whirl, and a caramel candied-peel bun."

"I'll bring them to your table," said the waitress, who had been looking at them with ill-concealed curiosity. But of course Peggy was known here.

"*Such* a long time," Peggy said now, settling down at the table by the window and casting a glance at the dingy street and the passing shoppers outside. "When was it? 'seventy-nine or 'eighty, I suppose. Just before we moved here to Romford."

And why did you do that, wondered Graham.

"Did you move to Milton Terrace then?"

"That's right. Of course it was my parents who bought it, and it's come down to me in the course of time. I wouldn't move now – unless I got a really good price for it. And then you've got to buy something for yourself to live in, haven't you? So really you're no better off."

"I never met your parents."

"Didn't you? One forgets. Dad had a good job in the motor trade. He died first, in 'ninety-three, and my mother two years later. They weren't old, not by a long chalk. His was heart, hers cancer. Life's a pig, isn't it?"

"It must be a bit lonely."

"Oh, not so you'd notice. I meant it was a pig for them. I manage very nicely."

They were interrupted by the waitress, bringing the coffees and the two rich cakes, side by side on a doily on a plate. They smiled at each other, but didn't talk till she was out of earshot.

"And you've got Christa, haven't you?"

No wonderment as to how he knew. Of course she knew all about the episode at Colchester.

"That's right. She's a lovely girl. They have so many freedoms we never had, don't they? But in the course of things she'll be moving out before very long."

"And you have a son too, don't you? Adam was it?"

She shot him a glance, but answered at once.

"That's right. He's fourteen. I don't expect *he'll* be moving out before he has to. They don't, boys. I've known mothers desperate to get rid of sons, but can't find a way to do it. As long as they can do what they want in the way of girlfriends, and get better cooking from their mothers, they stay put. It's a different world, isn't it?"

"It certainly is. Why did you tell Christa I was her father?" Graham had often found that in emotionally charged situations shock tactics worked well. Peggy bridled.

"Oh, I expect she got it all mixed up. You know what teenagers are like. Their hormones or testosterone or whatever it is are fizzing away inside them, and they don't know whether they're coming or going half the time."

Graham left a moment's silence. Peggy took advantage of it to start in on her second cake. It was the Viennese Whirl, and it left a lacy border of cream and chocolate around her lips. Suddenly for the second time Graham caught an intimation of the charm that had enthralled him as an adolescent and captured his soul for the months of rehearsal and performance of *St Joan*. He felt a cad for saying:

"Is it true that you were expecting a child when you moved here?"

Peggy put down her cake thoughtfully, and wiped her paper napkin around her lips. When she spoke she was almost schoolmistressy.

"Graham, we haven't got very long. You did say you hadn't got long, didn't you? And these are my friends here – the staff and the customers. Why should we talk about sad things in the past? Why would you want to embarrass me in front of my friends? Can't we let it drop? Promise?"

Graham thought, and then said:

"I promise."

She took up her cake again.

"And how did the reunion for poor old George Long go? He must be well past it by now."

"Past it? Not at all. Pretty much what he was when I was in 6C I thought. Just as commanding, just as theatrical."

"Well, he's damned lucky," she said forcefully. Then she retracted it with a charming smile. "Sorry. I shouldn't begrudge him it and it's mean of me, but I'd be very happy if I was the same girl as I was when you were in 6C."

"Wouldn't we all be happy to take twenty or thirty years off our ages?" Graham asked. "Though I always think children face things now that we never had inklings about when we were growing up. Having sex in one's early teens with parents turning a blind eye isn't just a joyful liberation."

"Of course it's not," said Peggy softly. Then she added: "Remember your promise."

"George I believe is still acting and directing – all sorts of things from Shakespeare to Music Hall…I wonder how good *St Joan* was. It was wonderful to be in, even a small part. And everyone seemed to think it was pretty good, and enjoyed it. So I suppose that must mean that it hit the mark. How you ever learnt the central role I can't imagine. It must have taken over your life."

She had finished eating, and was gazing ahead of her, with traces of chocolate still enchantingly clinging to her upper lip and chin.

"It did," she said dreamily. "In the most wonderful way. There's never been another year like it – never."

"And yet St Joan was not your part, in a way, was it?"

She shot him a glance.

"Remember your promise," she repeated, her voice once again soft and low. "You forget that St Joan is someone all the characters are interested in, are fascinated by. A bit mannish, direct and almost brutal at times, but always the centre of attention. Who says sex doesn't come into their fascination? I knew everyone else in the cast had – well, I suppose the current expression is 'got the hots' for me. The only female part in the play. Even *Macbeth* has a couple of other women's parts apart from the Lady. I was on my own, in my element, with everyone lusting after me. It was lovely – and disturbing!"

"I bet it was."

She suddenly wiped away a tear.

"And now I'm an assistant in a glorified corner shop, employed by a couple who are lovely people, good to me, and high up in the theatre scene here, but who are also the sort of people who give the tag 'do-gooder' a bad name. Isn't life a bugger?" She got up and turned to the door. "I must be getting back."

She waited at the door while Graham paid, then walked him briskly along the road.

"We must keep in touch," said Graham.

"Must we? You know my address, I gather. I suppose you have my telephone number as well. If you want to get in touch you can. From things you've said it doesn't seem likely you'll want to."

"There's the matter of —" began Graham. She put her finger to her lips, and his voice faded away. But as she turned to go back into Halliburton's she said, still in the same low voice:

"It was a boy, you know. A baby boy."

Then she went back into the shop, and her manner of shutting the door – theatrically, finally – told Graham their first encounter as adults was at an end. As he walked back to the car he found he did not regret it. That first sight of her through the window of the greengrocery shop had been deceptive: a sudden jump back in time had occurred, and he had been the sexually-hungry boy lusting for the loveliest thing on offer. But no sooner had they started talking than the cautious adult that he had become reasserted himself.

He did not entirely trust Peggy.

Perhaps he shouldn't have trusted her all those years ago. Perhaps she had been a sexual tease then – though a less experienced one. Who had she...'been with', as prim ladies used to say, during the rehearsal period and performance run of the play? Surely some talk must have reached his ears, low down though he was in the pecking order of the actors. What had happened after the meeting with her by the church at Upper Melrose and the days after that?

When he got home he picked up the phone and rang George Long.

"Hello, George. It's Graham Broadbent here."

George never forgot a pupil, never had to be prompted as to who they were or what they'd done.

"Young Broadbent! It was good to see you at the bean-feast. Honoured you could find the time to come. What can I do for you?"

"Ah…" So George had known from the tone of his voice that this wasn't a social call. That's what came of directing plays: all the social resonances of ordinary talk were registered. "Will you keep what I'm going to ask you strictly under your hat?" he said cautiously.

"Of course. Always do. Silent as the grave."

"Peggy Webster. Peggy Somers that was."

"Thought it might be something to do with her. Her name was in the air at dinner."

"It was. I want to know where she lived, and what her father did. I'm sure I knew at the time, but I never met them and it's all gone out of my mind."

"No reason for it to stay there, was there? The family lived in Bidford. Her father had a garage there. Not very prosperous. People passed through the village in their cars, but they kept on to somewhere bigger where the petrol would be cheaper. They'll be long gone, you know. They moved to Romford rather quickly. If they hadn't I'd have snapped her up for my Hermione the following year, instead of that puddingy girl who actually played her. You should try Romford, though it's pretty big – much more difficult than Bidford to find people in."

"Oh, I've done Romford, George. Peggy and I had coffee this morning. Time has changed her – you wouldn't know about time. But it's her background I'm interested in, purely for the purposes of a book, of course."

"Oh naturally, for fictional reasons. Well, don't worry: I'll be silent as the grave."

Graham wondered whether he would be. When it came down to it, a schoolboy never *knew* his masters. George could be the biggest old gossip in the business for all he knew.

4

Roots

The village of Bidford lay on the border of Essex and Suffolk fifty miles from London and eight miles from Lavenham, straggling either side of a road that was no longer important but still attracted a fair bit of traffic in the spring and summer: tourist trade, mostly families and old age couples in search of Picturesque Essex. There was a corner shop which doubled as a Post Office, and among the postcards strategically situated by the counter there were two or three Constable paintings, none of them of Bidford. The cottages along and just off the main street were suitably sized for the elderly, less so for young and growing families, though there were one or two more spacious dwellings, once the homes of the rector, the doctor and a solicitor who practised elsewhere. The last was the only one who remained, as if he alone answered to an eternal need, but the Rectory was home to a Colchester businessman, and the doctor's house was weekend home to a psychiatrist in regular demand for daytime television and radio, a fount of instant diagnosis and advice.

There was one pub, The Haywain, previously the King's Head, with Constable's wagon now on the inn-sign, in place of George III, who was too unromantic to attract passing custom. Shunning the tearooms, which seemed exclusively geared up to the tourist trade, Graham picked on The Haywain for his lunch, with a menu of staple English fare such as scampi, baked potato with chili con carne and lasagne. As he parked the car Graham realized that he had driven through the village from end to end, but had seen no sign of a garage. Garages, like electric razors and plastic macs, had become things of the past.

The Haywain, that lunchtime, was populated mainly by locals, by old and new residents. They were dressed casually, even sloppily, but they were yarning to each other, or to the landlord, swapping comments on the weather, the harvest, or the political situation and – on his entry through the saloon bar door – fixing their eyes on the newcomer. Yes, mainly local: that was ideal.

"I'll have a pint of Bass…and the lasagne as well. You can dispense with the salad."

"No salad? Will you have the chips then?"

"Oh, all right. With chips." Arnold Wesker had been right all those years ago. It was chips with everything for the British. The landlord bustled off to the kitchen with the order, then came back to do his landlordly duties by the newcomer.

"You a stranger round here?" he asked, as he drew his pint. Graham nodded.

"I am now, though I'm just over the border in Suffolk. I grew up in Colchester. I'm near Ipswich now, but I'm having a day off to drive round old haunts. To tell you the truth, I'm not sure that I was ever in Bidford as a boy."

"Lots of folk pass through here," said the landlord.

"I can see that. I had a girlfriend here once, briefly, but I can't recall that I ever visited her at home. I think her father had a garage here."

The all-male customer clientele looked at each other.

"Well," said the man immediately beside Graham at the bar, "that would have to be either Ted Somers or Wilf Bradby, who bought it off him. Going by your age, that is, which I'd guess as early or mid-forties."

"Pretty spot-on," said Graham, swallowing his dislike of people who guessed his age and got it right. "It was Ted

Somers. I never met him, so far as I recall – which means I was never 'taken home to meet the parents'."

"That would be Peggy you were going with, then," said the man. "She had one or two boyfriends that she didn't take home to meet the parents. She was the apple of their eye. She'd want to be very sure before she took anyone home, because they'd have hit the roof if he hadn't been up to scratch."

"Meaning nothing personal," said the landlord hastily. "Where's your manners, Percy?"

"Sorry," said the man, not noticeably shame-faced. "Nothing personal at all. I'm Percy Sharp. I've lived here pretty much all my life, though I worked in Lavenham. We all remember the garage, because it was convenient. But neither Ted nor Wilf could make a go of it. Wilf sold it five years after he took it over. See the new houses next door to this place? That's where the garage was."

Graham nodded. He'd wondered whether that was the case.

"Owning a garage hasn't been much of a recipe for success for years now," he said. "Ted must have seen the signs at the beginning of the trend."

"Happen. But I don't think he'd have moved if it hadn't been for Peggy. I'd better not say any more. Nobody really knows the facts. And for all I know you could be the father."

There was a sniggering around the bar.

"For someone who isn't going to say anything, Percy Sharp, you get your meaning across," said the landlord.

"If she was pregnant when she moved away," lied Graham, "then I wasn't the father. We had a brief little romantic friendship about eighteen months before the family moved away. Do you remember Peggy, Percy?"

"Aye, I remember her. And her brief romantic friendships. Proper little bobby-dazzler she was. Talented too. They say she was a brilliant little actress. Played St Theresa or something in a school play. Ted and Mary were over the moon."

"It was St Joan. I was in the play too."

"Were you though?" said Percy, looking at him appraisingly, like a tailor. "Wouldn't have put you down as the acting type."

"Small part."

"Anyway, we heard nothing but that play for months. I mind her father talking about her, standing where you're stood now. Boring the pants off us, if the truth be known, but we all liked her, and could see she was something out of the ordinary. Still…"

Graham waited, but nothing came.

"Still?" he was forced to ask.

"Still, talent isn't everything, is it? Anyone who's had children, or had to do with them, knows that. You think one of them's the brightest knife in the box, and then something happens and they spend the rest of their lives in dull jobs that go nowhere. And sometimes it's nothing that happens, but them just reaching their top, the limits of their talents, and not being able to push themselves any further up."

"Was that the case with Peggy? She reached her top?"

"Oh no. Something happened. I suppose I've more or less told you what that was, haven't I?"

"Yes, you have."

"That wasn't the official line. According to her dad and mum she'd had the offer of a place in Drama School. As a consequence they were moving closer to London – Romford it was – so she could take it up and still live at home."

"Yes, I knew they went to Romford."

"Oh, you heard, did you? That at least was true. Dicky Mortlake – we buried him ten years since – was driving through Romford a few months after they upped sticks and left, and he saw Peggy walking with her mother, very pregnant. So that was what it was, which frankly was what we'd all guessed anyway."

"Had you just guessed that because she was pretty and young, and just the age to be careless about precautions?" asked Graham, lapsing into the circumlocutions of his youth.

"Partly, maybe," said Percy, remembering. "But she was always…flighty."

He looked as if he wanted to say no more, but Graham pressed him.

"Had lots of boyfriends?"

"Aye, she did, but that wasn't what I was thinking about. Her manner was…let's say it wasn't modest, not what we expected then from a schoolgirl. I said she was flighty. I think I mean she was flirtatious. She'd come at you with little remarks and double meanings and sexual provocations – even when she was with much older men, like me. Mostly we made a joke of it, but who's to know whether there weren't some who fell for it. The father of the child could have been one of the boyfriends of her own age, but equally it could have been any man in the village, most of us included."

"Did her parents know nothing about her ways?"

"'Course not. Can see you haven't got teenage children. The parents always get duped – I expect it's been going on since the Garden of Eden. Peggy never did anything while they were by. She was Mary Poppins or Maria von Trapp when they were around. To this day Ted has never said who the father was – or even whether he knows who the father was. That's how much he and Mary were hurt and surprised by it."

Graham stopped, his pint half way up to his mouth. He looked around at the other men at the bar.

"But Peggy's father's dead, isn't he?"

"Not so far as we know," said Percy Sharp, and they all shook their heads. "Her mother, Mary, died two years ago, but we'd have heard if Ted had gone. He and Mary used to come back every year or two, just to visit Kath Moores, who was Mary's great friend. Ted was back last summer on his own. Kath would have told people if he'd died."

Graham was conscious he was being looked at by the landlord.

"Do you know what I think?" the man said.

"No."

"I think you've just met up again with Peggy Somers – or whatever her new name is. She's brought back a lot of memories of an old love affair. And she's spun you a lot of stories about herself and her activities, just like she used to tell us."

Graham was pleased to feel that the atmosphere had lightened. Everyone was grinning.

"Well, your guess comes pretty close. Yes, I have met Peggy again. But why on earth would she tell me her father was dead when he's not?"

One or two of the men shrugged.

"Who can tell?" one of them said. "Sometimes she'd tell you stories that had her mingling with celebrities: she'd met Johnny Rotten or Laurence Olivier had come to see her in that school play. You knew she was making that sort of thing up, and why. She found life humdrum and limited here, and she was yearning for bright lights and glamour. So she made up another existence for herself."

"But she made up stories you couldn't see any reason for," said Percy Sharp, unwilling to lose the limelight. "She'd tell you her mother had an incurable illness, or that her cat had been killed by someone's dog – and it was, like, childish. You saw the cat next time you walked down the street. It was as if she thought we were stupid."

"Or the fact that getting our attention, or sympathy, for that moment, was all that mattered," put in the other man.

"What you're saying is that she is a congenital fantasist," said Graham.

"A born liar is how we'd probably put it," said Percy.

"But charming with it," put in his feed. "Oodles of pathos, or come-hither, or whatever role she was playing that day. And we were pleased and flattered. We were middle-aged men, and it was nice having a fresh and pretty young thing making up to us, and telling us things. You're that age yourself. You'd be flattered too."

I was, thought Graham. By her daughter.

"Here's your lasagne," said the landlord, seeing his wife coming through from the back with a plate bearing a microwaved casserole dish with chips around it. "Would you like it at a table?"

"I'd better. But if anyone has any information about Peggy or her parents that hasn't come up yet, I'd be interested to hear."

Graham settled down on a sofa under a light and tucked in to a better-than-expected lasagne. He took out that day's *Times*, but kept it turned to the First Night arts pages, periodically flicking his eyes to the little knot of male figures by the bar. He had no doubt they were talking about Peggy Somers, or more likely the family as a whole. Graham kept on stolidly eating, surprised at how hungry he was, now and then sighing over the arts reviews. His definition of old age was when you found a paper's arts pages contained mostly things you didn't consider art at all. And he had reached that stage by the age of forty-four. As he mopped up the last of the meat and pasta and the chips he was not surprised when he was approached by a man who detached himself from the little group at the bar. It was not Percy Sharp, but a short, slight man who had taken little part in the talk thus far.

"Do you mind if I sit down? I'm Ben Coward, by the way. I didn't catch your name?"

"I didn't give it. Graham Broadbent."

The man wrinkled his forehead.

"Rings a bell somehow."

"I write books. Novels. I get into the Colchester papers sometimes."

"Best keep quiet about the novels. The others over there are a bit suspicious. We like our privacy. They weren't willing to come and talk to you, but we thought there was something you ought to know."

"Well, thank you for taking the risk."

"Oh, not really a risk," Ben Coward said, afraid he had been too melodramatic. "But Kath Moores is a strong-minded lady. Formidable, one might say. I'd rather you didn't —"

"Of course. I've never been a journalist, but never revealing your sources seems a good idea for people generally."

"She's not really a dragon, but she's rather a strict, straight-laced person, and very private. Methodist…We think Ted Somers and she may be – what shall I say? – getting together. Like we told you, he's been visiting on his own here, and Kath has had several weekends away. She doesn't tell anyone where she's been, and if anyone asks she says 'Visiting friends'."

"I see."

"Now, if anyone brings up Peggy's name, for years Ted's just said 'We don't talk about her', clenching his mouth, and Mary, his dead wife, has done the same."

"That could be the illegitimate child."

"Oh, I don't mean that long. The child's birth would be

coming up to twenty-five years ago now. They'd talk about Peggy quite naturally for years after that, once they started coming back here. No, it would be about ten years since they clammed up about her. And if the name has come up recently, Kath has done the same."

"Sounds like a complete rift."

"That's our feeling. We think it would be worth your while to pay Kath a visit."

"I'm thinking the same."

"Number twenty-two, along the street here."

And the little man slipped off his stool and went back to the bar.

Graham wiped his mouth with the paper napkin, drained the last of his pint, and took the glass over to the bar. Eyes followed his every movement. He thanked them all, casually, for their help, and then strolled out into the September sunshine.

He found number twenty-two quite easily. He rang, and when the door opened he found himself regarded closely as he stammered out his self-introduction.

"Mrs Moores? You won't know me, but it was suggested —"

He was met by a strong stare through surprisingly up-to-the-minute spectacles.

"At the Haywain, yes. I saw you arriving there an hour ago. They're a lot of old women, those who collect there at lunchtime – nothing but gossips, and what they find to gossip about day after day heaven only knows. But come in. I think I can guess what it's about."

"Really?"

"Now I see you up close I think you must be Graham Broadbent."

He came straight into her sitting room, which had no hallway between it and the High Street, and looked at her in surprise.

"Did you recognise me from my dust-jackets? It's such an old photo I thought —"

"Yes, I have read your books, two or three of them. But I knew the name before that, and looking at you I can see that you're roughly of an age with Peggy."

"Ah yes. It was Peggy I came to talk about."

"Yes. There's not many topics of conversation in this village, like I said, so Peggy and the Somerses have lasted a long time, even though they've been gone from here now twenty-five years or more."

"But you've always kept in touch with them?"

"Oh yes, by letters and through visits. You'll have been told that in The Haywain. Mary was my best friend in the village, and I've kept in touch with Ted since she died. That will certainly have been told you by those awful old women in there."

"I'm a bit bewildered," said Graham slowly. "I've talked to Peggy recently, and she said both her parents were dead, and had been for some time."

Mrs Moores considered, then said.

"I don't think we're going to get anywhere if we circle round and round what Peggy has said, or why. What she says has very little connection with reality. She's had little or nothing to do with either of her parents since she got the house off them."

Graham shot her a quick glance.

"Is that phrase 'got the house off them' significant? Was that the cause of the breach between them?"

"Yes, it was. By then she had Christa and Adam, and she wanted space. She persuaded Ted and Mary to move out to a bungalow, and said she'd pay the market price for the house. What she in fact paid was about half that, and some of that was a loan from her brother which she never paid back. She relied on them not suing or calling in the police, and of course they didn't. She'd been the apple of their eye when she was growing up – much more than her brother. So they couldn't bear to wash the family dirty linen in public, and they just broke off relations with her. And that suited *her* very well, and hurt *them* very much."

"Didn't they see the grandchildren at all?"

"Christa has been going round fairly regularly since she was about sixteen. Adam goes with her now and then. It's better than nothing. Ted values it, specially now he's on his own. He's retired as well, so he's lonely, and time hangs heavy. We're thinking of getting married, but nothing's decided yet. It's a big step at my age, with my husband having been dead thirty years. You get used to your independence if you are widowed at an early age. Ted is too old to do that."

Graham felt he was trespassing too long on her time and her memories, but one thing still bothered him.

"You said you knew my name before you read any of my books."

"Well, yes. Your name came up between us – me and the Somerses."

"When was that? Was it when Christa was born?"

"Christa? Why would you think that? That was much later. No, it came up at the time when they felt they had to move from this village. When Peggy was eighteen and pregnant. It was still quite a big disgrace in those days."

"So she had a child then, did she? Why has she told Christa that I'm her father?"

Kath Moores raised her eyebrows and thought.

"Because you're famous, and she doesn't want to lose the prestige of having...gone with you."

"But the baby itself?"

"She had it adopted, of course. So it's not around to be boasted to about its famous father."

"And the baby was? —"

"A boy."

"That's what she told me. That at least was true."

"Oh, she mingles truth with the rest. It makes it seem that it's all true. You'd really do best to avoid her altogether, you know. She's trouble, that girl – woman."

"If she had my son without even telling me, I don't know whether I can do that," said Graham sadly.

5

Starting Again

Graham almost had to rub his eyes when it happened again. He opened the front door and there she was.

"Hello, Graham. Are you going to ask me in this time?"

The background was the familiar one of a street in Hepton Magna rather than a hotel corridor, but she was exactly the same. And he felt a surge of pleasure at seeing her again. There was now no suspicion or scepticism, nor any fear at all. There was a surge of that well-recognised lust, but also something that, for him was so much rarer: that other four-letter word beginning with 'l'.

"Of course. Come in."

She marched confidently in, through to his living room, then looked around her appraisingly.

"Nice!"

Graham was quite aware, as perhaps Christa was not, of an undertone that qualified the praise: 'not much personality' seemed to be the doubt expressed in her tone. He decided they shouldn't go into all that. As far as he was concerned personality was something to be kept submerged. He just said: "Thanks."

She turned to him, smiling a little satirically.

"So why did you invite me in this time without my having to force you into it?"

"There was one word that you said last time but didn't say this time."

"Yeah, well, we'd better talk about that."

"In a minute. Would you like coffee?"

"Tea, if that's all right."

"Tea it is." He bustled out, but from the kitchen he shouted: "So who've you been talking to? Your mother?"

"Not much good talking to her. I expect you know why."

"Yes. She lies. But why did you believe her when she told you I was your father?"

"Because she's been telling me that ever since I was little."

Graham came back with cups and saucers and began setting them out on a coffee table.

"Fantasies are things people cling to," he said slowly. "Eventually some people come to believe them themselves. Though I don't think that's true in this case."

"Oh? Why not?"

"Because when I met her — you knew I had met her?"

"Oh yes. She told me about it, and said you were still desperately in love with her."

"Ha! Anyway, when I met her, and as she was saying goodbye, she just said that the baby was a boy."

He left her thoughtful as he went to make the tea. When he came back she asked immediately:

"The baby you were the father of?"

"Apparently."

"How old would he be now?"

"Middle twenties…Did you hear the truth from your grandfather?"

"Yes. I went round for a talk." She giggled but it was a troubled sound. "It's stupid — I was so surprised to hear that you weren't my father that I didn't ask him who was."

"Perhaps the grandparents were never told. Your mother could have been their only possible source of information, so they could have realized that anything she told them was suspect."

"Of course. Yes, I expect that's true. Well, if it's not you I don't know that I'm interested."

Graham thought this was a healthy reaction. Christa accepted a cup and sat sipping at it and nibbling a biscuit.

"This is nice. *This* is how I thought it would be in Colchester."

"How did you find out my address?"

"I'm doing a librarianship course at college."

"So you found it in *Twentieth Century Novelists*?"

"How did you know?"

"It's the only reference work that gives addresses. Are you really going to be a librarian?"

She shrugged, smiling.

"Oh, it's just one of my units. One of my 'mights'. I'm doing it with Art History and Ancient Egypt."

"Why Ancient Egypt?"

"It's there. I just fancied it. And the teacher, if you must know."

Graham sighed.

"I see. It's like a different world."

"Oh, don't go all 'older generation' on me. So what about this twenty-five-year-old baby, then?"

"What about him?"

"What happened to him?"

"Search me. I've been told he was put out for adoption."

"Aren't you interested?"

Graham thought.

"I suppose I am. I'm in an almighty muddle about him. I've only recently known anything about him. I did really get intrigued, though, when you turned up with the claim that I knew couldn't be true. Was there a baby who was not you? But actually getting interested in the baby as a young man – I don't know if I can – or should."

"The way you put it, it sounds as if you just saw me as a problem, a puzzle."

"Not true. Quite the reverse. But being interested in you did involve a problem, and I'm glad to have solved it."

"Leaving the other problem of little Incognito."

"I think 'Ignoto' might be a better name."

"What's that when it's at home?"

"'Unknown'. Our unknown quantity."

Christa nodded, now relaxed again.

"Sounds about right. Anyway, you can call him what you want. He's your son. There are places you can go, you know."

Graham frowned.

"To find out what happened to him? Adoption agencies, do you mean?"

"No, I meant on the Web. I've heard of a couple of sites. One's called 'Parents and Children', and I think there's another one called 'Find Your Family'."

"Wouldn't that depend on him wanting to get in touch with me?"

"Yeah. Or with mum. I've read that most of them want to contact their mothers."

"I suppose that's natural. Fathers are expendable things these days."

"I didn't think so. And I've still got that problem."

On an impulse Graham said:

"You'll stay for lunch, won't you? I was just going to have toasted cheese. Or we could go to the pub."

"I'd rather have it here. I make a mean Welsh Rarebit. Would you let me make it for us?"

"I'd be honoured. Come through to the kitchen. What do you need apart from bread and cheese?"

"I'll find everything. I'm an expert on other people's

kitchens. You go and read the paper and I'll bring it to you."

As Graham sat in his easy chair he thought he was being treated by Christa rather as she probably treated her grandfather. The idea made him feel oddly uneasy, and also sad. He tried to read the morning paper, but kept being distracted. He would have liked to go and see Christa finding her way round his kitchen, but could think of no way he could do that without being spotted. It was only ten minutes or so before Christa came back with odorous and still-sizzling plates.

"Your kitchen was a doddle. Everything in its place. I've never known an easier one, apart from boyfriends'. They're always so *boring*. No wonder most boys prefer to stay at home, when they've so little imagination when it comes to food."

Graham preferred not to think about Christa and boyfriends.

"I suppose your grandfather's is a kitchen you know well."

"Oh yes. I cosset Grandad when I go round to see him."

"What has he told you?"

Christa watched him tucking in greedily, thought, then replied.

"About my background? About Mother? Not very much, really. Like you said I don't think he and my grandma were told much about how I came into the world. I guess it was probably the same with little 'Ignoto'. Or perhaps what they were told was lies, and they realize that. About Mother, Grandad feels he has to be careful. He doesn't want to undermine her with her own children. I should think me and Adam know more about her than he does. He and Grandma seem to have worn rose-coloured spectacles all the time she was growing up, and then lost them in a big way."

"It was that time I was wondering about...This Welsh

Rarebit is marvellous. I could never make it as well."

"Mum's recipe. Didn't she ever make it for you?"

"She never made me a meal. It wasn't that sort of relationship. We were very young, and it was very short."

"Gran and Grandad never said much about that time. When I talked to Grandad he said giving up the baby for adoption was 'for the best'. He and Grandma may have taken the initiative, but I got the impression that Mum was happy to go along with it."

They ate companionably for some time in silence. When Graham had finished he put his cutlery on his plate, then suddenly burst out:

"Why should I want to find this *son*?"

Christa looked at him, surprised.

"Why wouldn't you? I thought every man wanted a son."

"I never knew I had a son till your mother told me. I didn't miss having one, I didn't feel incomplete without one. I didn't ache to believe your mother was speaking the truth."

"Oh, she was. Grandad definitely said that the baby was a 'he'."

"Does everything your mother says have to be double-checked?"

"Pretty much. Most of the time we've learnt – Adam and me – to ignore her. She tells us things, and we just say 'oh yes?' and get on with our lives. It's only if what she says is something major – like a new man moving in with us – that we take any notice."

"I see. It seems a curious upbringing."

"I suppose it has been, in a way. I sometimes hear other people talking about their home life and I think: 'You've had it easy.' Then I think: 'You've got it dull too.'" She laughed. "My mum's never been dull, I can say that for her."

"All this isn't answering my question. What use do I have for a son?"

"I can't answer that for you. But couldn't we just wait and find out if we can identify him? Then you can think it over and decide if you want to meet him."

"But by then I'll feel I'm already committed."

"You won't be, though. To meeting him, maybe, but not to anything else."

"Emotionally I will be committed. I don't think people should be played with. And I might have to go through the motions of being interested in someone I find thoroughly boring and antipathetic, just because of a ten-day fling back in 1979."

"Is that all it was?"

"Yes. Three or four individual days when we met up and…you know. So what is there in it for me? Come to that, what is there in it for him?"

"Well," said Christa, clearing up the plates, "I know what *I'd* want if I were him. And you can't know what's in it for either of you unless you actually meet up, can you?"

Graham helped her, ran some water in the sink, and together they washed up the pots from breakfast and lunch. All the time he was thinking what a sensible girl she was, how adult, as well as how lovely. When they were finished Christa began collecting up her things.

"Time I was going. You'll be wanting some time to write."

Graham could have told her that he didn't write in the afternoon, and that he wasn't writing anything at the moment anyway. But he didn't. He did want to be alone, he did want time to think.

"We must keep in touch," he said. "I've got your mother's telephone number. When's the best time to ring – when she won't be there?"

"Friday evening is late opening at the shop. I cook a meal for when she comes back just after seven, even if I'm heading out later"

"Maybe I should have your grandfather's address."

"I suppose so. Though if you do go and see him I should probably come with you. But why would you go and see him except to find out more about your son?" she added with a sly smile on her face.

Graham felt he'd walked into a trap.

"I suppose there might be some tiny itch of curiosity and paternal interest. Anyway, it occurs to me that I'm being selfish. Whatever I may feel, you very likely are interested in an elder brother you've never seen. And if you want to make contact there's nothing in the world I could or would do to stop you."

"True. And yes – I am curious. And if he wants to find his mother, I could help him."

"Would that go down well with Peggy?"

That brought Christa up short. She frowned.

"Do you know, I've no idea. Why should she not want to be found?"

"Is she afraid of ageing? A twenty-five-year-old son suddenly appearing puts a few more years on her age than a nineteen-year-old daughter."

"Oh, I think she'd get over those feelings quite quickly. She'd probably like the novelty of the situation, especially as she'd be the centre of attention."

"So I'd imagine. You know we met when we were both in a school play, don't you?"

"Yes, Grandad told me that."

"She had testosterone-stoked young men around her for those three months, all lusting after her like crazy. That's probably where she got the thirst for being the centre of attention."

"Do you think? I'd have thought she became an amateur actress *because* of liking the limelight."

She's really very sharp, thought Graham. Or has learnt a lot from her upbringing. At the door she kissed him.

"A chaste kiss from your non-daughter," she said. "And we'll keep in touch."

She made it sound very inviting.

It was over a week before Graham heard from Christa again. He found the days long and empty. It was ridiculous to have become dependent on seeing or hearing from someone he had initially regarded as a threat, but there it was…He told himself now and then that he was just curious to know whether Christa had turned up any facts about the boy who was his son, but he knew that was not so. It was Christa herself, her personality, her enthusiasm for life, that he missed.

One day, when he was out, she left a message on his answer-machine. It just consisted of "Love you, Christa." Not very sustaining in itself, but it gave him the sound of her voice, and he didn't wipe the message. He thought it was a lovely voice – a joyful, heart-lifting voice. The voice of an actress's daughter. He thought about Peggy, and her parents' story about her having won a scholarship to one of the drama schools. What wonderful things might have happened if it had been true! What rich pleasure she might have brought to theatre-goers, television watchers and cineastes up and down the country. He was convinced, like everybody in *St Joan*, not just that she had talent, but that it was a peerless talent, that with training she could have stood alone among actresses of her generation.

Now he heard the same notes in the voice of her daughter.

He wondered, like her, who Christa's father was. Someone quite ordinary, probably. But not him, anyway. That was a cause for satisfaction and relief. Christa was not his. So anything else was possible.

She rang him nine days after coming to see him.

"I think things are beginning to happen," she said.

"*What* things are beginning to happen?"

"You *know*." And of course he did know. He was only playing for time. To decide how he should act. "My big brother. The one who should have been around as I was growing up to defend me from school bullies and teach me how to smoke."

"You mean my only son," said Graham quietly.

"Yeah – that too. You *are* interested, whatever you pretend. There's been a message on the Find Your Family website. It's looking for a woman who had a baby in the Romford area in the Spring of 1980. Possible names: Summers or Somers."

"And what's his name?"

"Terence John Telford."

"Doesn't ring any bells."

"Why would it, if he was given up for adoption?"

"No, of course it wouldn't."

"Mum probably never knew the name of the couple who adopted him. Weren't the authorities pretty strict then?"

"I don't know. I know nothing about it myself, remember. I was certainly not kept informed. But you're probably right about the authorities. Anything else?"

"Well there's something that's a bit odd. He gives the date of his own birth as 5.15.80."

"What? – Oh, I see."

"The American way. Meaning the fifteenth of May – what we'd write as 15.5.80. And he spells 'favour' as 'F.A.V.O.R'. He asks anyone who might have any information about his mother 'as a favor' to write to Terence John Telford at his address."

"What is his address?"

"Somewhere in Wimbledon."

Graham was silent.

"The spelling could just be a typo, but taken with the date, and his wanting to know about a baby born in Spring '80…This seems to be the man we are after, and he apparently has some kind of American connection."

"The family who adopted him could have gone out there to live, or to work temporarily, at some time while he was growing up."

"They could. That became much more frequent in the Eighties."

"*Well*?" Graham was silent, thinking, so Christa amended that to: "Are you interested?"

"Yes. Yes, I think I am."

"So what do I do?"

"Does he give an ordinary postal address?"

"Yes – the one in Wimbledon."

"Of course. Well, couldn't you write to him briefly, say there is a Margaret (Peggy) Somers at Milton Terrace who you believe had an illegitimate son at about the time he's interested in, and leave it at that? Send it ordinary mail, so as to be more private."

"So that's what you think I should do, is it?"

"Yes, I think that would be the right thing."

"Good. Because that's what I've already done."

6

Together at Last

"Graham, I think we should meet."

It was pure pleasure to be called Graham.

"Sure. What's happened? Has contact been made?"

"Yes, it has. He's been for a visit."

"He moves fast."

"Very. You'd think they'd known each other for years."

"You saw him, then?"

"Oh yes. I wasn't meant to, but I did."

"I bet you did. What were your impressions?"

There was a silence.

"I think we should meet again, Graham. This is all complicated. He's my brother, and presumably your son. Ten or twelve words on the telephone don't seem enough."

"Of course you're right." Graham was surprised but impressed by her compunction. "Suggest somewhere where we could meet."

"Could it be London? Not Romford. Proper London?"

"Proper London would be fine. Where should it be? Green Park is nice at this time of year."

"Green Park on Thursday at three p.m.?"

"Fine. Why Thursday?"

"Thursday afternoon's my free day at College."

Graham noted that she hadn't asked if Thursday was a free day for him too. He rather liked the idea that she was taking control. Perhaps she was the sort of woman who always would.

Green Park on Thursday at 2.55 was looking beautiful, but it was also looking crowded. There were empty seats, but how long would they remain empty if he and Christa sat on one of them? Even before she arrived Graham had decided they would sit on the grass. She walked down from the tube station, immensely self-assured. Graham kissed her in a step-fatherly sort of way, and then led her towards a tree, spreading shade around it which would probably keep most of the sun-worshippers in the park away. Christa nodded her agreement with his choice.

"Yes, we need to be on our own," she said, with the gravity of an adult. "Not that I have anything very scandalous to report —"

"But we do need to be private," agreed Graham. "Afterwards I thought we might go to tea at the Ritz if you'd like that."

"Is that something special?"

"Very much so."

"Then I'd like it very much!"

He liked her naiveté, but he also liked her quickness in picking up the implications of his words. When they had settled down and Christa had taken a Crunchie bar from her bag and contentedly worked her way through it, remarking that tea was some way away, she consciously ordered her thoughts, a process that was clearly visible in her young, impressionable face, then began.

"Right. Well, I told you I wrote this young man a note telling him about Mum. I gave a fictitious name, and said he could contact me through Darren Clarkson, that's my boyfriend. He didn't. He must have checked Mum's name and address though, probably through the telephone directory. He contacted her direct, I think it must have been last Tuesday, early on before she went to work, because when I got home in the evening after College, she was very not-with-it and disturbed. I dropped in at Halliburton's – that's the greengrocer's – the next afternoon and they said she'd been acting odd all the day before. So I reckon he must have rung her, told her that he was the baby boy she'd given away twenty-five years ago, and talked over what had happened to him, what he'd done, in those years."

"That sounds likely enough," said Graham.

"And Peggy – I often call her that – was naturally a bit shaken by that. They must have left it open if and when they'd meet, because it was a few days later before she began making hints that she'd like me out of the house on Monday evening. "Why, have you got a new man coming round?" I asked. She wasn't embarrassed or anything – she's beyond that – but she just said 'sort of', and went on insisting I find something to do on Monday evening. Finally I said I'd go along to my friend Josie's, to put in some work on a college project I said we were doing."

Graham was silent. He still found it difficult to imagine the mental state of children whose mothers (or fathers, come to that) had a succession of partners. Flashing across his brain came an image of his mother at the sink washing up, or with a headscarf knotted around her hair, trotting off to the shops to get something nice for the family's tea. He just nodded.

"Anyway, Monday came, and after college I had some tea and then made a big show of getting books together for the project. I took all the impressive ones, and when Mum asked what the project was I said it was 'interdisciplinary'. That floored her. Anyway, when she began to get nervy (it doesn't take much these days) I waved her goodbye, left the house, and settled down in a garden four doors down, where the house is vacant and up for sale."

"So as to catch a glimpse of him?"

"Yeah, and I didn't have to wait long. You know Milton Terrace don't you?"

"Yes, I've been there."

"I know. Mrs Poulson next door told me about this man asking after Mum, and I guessed it was you. Anyway, not many people come along it apart from the residents, and certainly not in the evening. So it didn't take much detective skill to work out that the young man walking along looking at numbers was Terence John Telford."

"What was he like?"

"Not like you. Not like Mum either, come to that."

"No reason why he should be. I'd have said that people who looked like either of their parents were the exception rather than the rule."

"I've never really thought about it. Adam doesn't look like either of his. I think I'm a *bit* like Mum, though *only* in looks. I'm not at all like her in character."

"You prefer truth to fantasy?"

She thought.

"Yes, I prefer the truth."

"You still haven't told me what this young man *did* look like."

"Well, he looks his age: mid-twenties. If you'd asked me to guess, that's what I'd have said. He's a lot bigger than you, quite wide across the shoulders, but there's a lot of flesh there. I like my men skinnier. He's probably an inch or two taller than you, and he's got these chubby cheeks, wavy dark hair, and he kind of looks – I don't know…"

"What?"

"Of being, on top, rather smug, though underneath I think he's rather confused."

"You got a lot out of a brief glimpse."

"Oh, but I didn't have *just* a glimpse…I let him go by, and saw him go into number twenty-five. Then I just sat and waited for a half hour or so. I didn't want to interrupt their long-overdue reunion."

"Sensitive of you, if rather cynically expressed."

"That about sums up my feelings about Mum. I could have imagined that she might be pleased and emotional about the whole thing, but she's never mentioned him. So that I couldn't believe that he meant very much to her."

"But eventually you invented an excuse for going back, I assume?"

"Of course. I gave them plenty of time to take the first steps, then I walked back home, let myself in, shouted 'Sorry, I forget a book', and went straight upstairs. I nearly shouted 'I won't interrupt', which I would have done if it had been one of Peggy's men who was there, but I definitely did intend to interrupt, so luckily I didn't. As it turned out, when I came downstairs with a book in my hand (I'd left my bag with all the other books in it down by the gate), there he was in the door of the sitting room. He came forward with his hand out. 'Hi!,' I said. 'I'm Christa Webster, Peggy's daughter.' He shook my hand. 'I'm Terry Telford,' he said. 'I'm Peggy's son. Your elder brother'."

"Did you act surprised?"

"If I did, I didn't do it convincingly. Mum was behind the sitting room door, watching us. She said, like she was accusing me: 'You *knew*. Knew about Terry. Someone told you.' Poor Terry was starting to look really confused by this time. She said 'It must be that blasted father of mine. Though he and Mum were very keen to keep it quiet at the time, and I thought they had since as well…I'm pretty sure Graham never knew, but you've met him recently, and I did sort of…' And Terry said: 'Who's Graham?' Peggy didn't reply directly. She just took him in her arms and said: 'I think there've been enough surprises for one evening, don't you, Terry darling?'"

"I can see her point," said Graham.

"Yeah, I guess. Better not make a meal of it. Anyway,
Mother gave me a warning look, meaning I should make
myself scarce, so I thought I'd stay a little longer. I looked at
Terry and said: 'So where have you been all my life?' which was
really aimed at *her* not him. He smiled, a bit awkwardly, and
said he'd been with his adoptive parents, and they'd gone to
America for a while, but now they were home again, and so
was he. I said: 'Are you still living with your parents?' and he
said no, he'd moved out, and was doing supply teaching."

"Supply teaching? That can be tough. Is he doing it in the
London area? I should think that's tantamount to slow
suicide."

"I think it's in London," said Christa, thoughtfully. "His
parents live in Wimbledon, and he used their address when he
posted his appeal on the Internet. He says he's trying to get his
American degree recognised here, then he'll apply for
permanent jobs."

"Well, that fills in the gaps," said Graham. "Anything else?"

"When I refused to go, or rather just stood there, he and
Peggy disappeared into the kitchen, where she was making one
of her delicious little suppers for him, just as if he was one of
her fancy men (that's what she calls them, unless she's got
hopes that they will become something more permanent).
They began getting – not lovey-dovey exactly, but sort of
giggly, almost flirting, and a bit embarrassing to watch."

"Young people always do get embarrassed by age
differences," said Graham, a touch of bitterness entering his
tone. Christa's face betrayed irritation.

"I *don't*. I'm old-fashioned. I like older men myself, and that
seems perfectly natural. Somehow I just can't see a young man

getting the hots for an older woman."

"That's a horrible expression," said Graham. "I expect you got it from the Australian soaps."

"I'm not wised up about etymology," said Christa, her tone becoming satirical. "Do you really watch *Home and Away* and *Neighbours*? I can't imagine it."

"Just now and then. One has to keep up with what young people are watching."

"You should keep up with what young people are doing and thinking – what their lives are like."

She sounded like a schoolmistress of an earlier age.

"I sometimes wonder whether they have a real life at all," said Graham.

"Cynic. You know nothing about it." Christa got up. "Come on. It's time to see what real life is like. Take me to the tea room at the Ritz."

Graham had had tea at the Ritz before, but not often. He was delighted to see that Christa was wide-eyed. He had booked a table, and the head waiter said: "Ah yes, Mr Broadbent – delighted to see you, sir." Christa took this to mean that her companion had been recognised, but Graham suspected that the name had been registered, and the man was hedging his bets in case he turned out to be the reasonably-well-known novelist. They sat down and surveyed the menu of traditional goodies. Christa expressed a healthy distaste for Earl Grey, but let Graham select from the remaining teas, and herself chose greedily from the list of edibles. When the order had been taken, Graham sat back in his chair, saw that all the tables nearby were deep in conversation or social chit-chat, then said softly:

"And is that all that happened when Terry came a-visiting?"

"Pretty much," said Christa. "While they got more and

more mother-and-son, I decided to slip out. I did drop in on
Josie, and came back home at the agreed time. Mother was on
her own, mooning around the house. She had a bit of a go at
me for coming back earlier, but she was in such a good,
dreamy mood that it was like water off a duck's back. I tried
to get into a discussion about my new brother, but she sailed
off to bed singing 'You are my heart's delight,' which was one
of my gran's favourites. My granny Somers, that is, who died,
not my granny Webster in Stanway, who is my stepfather's
mother. I've always been closer to her than I was to my
stepfather."

"And that was it, was it?"

"Pretty much. A bit later Adam came back, I told him what
had happened, and he went ballistic."

"Adam. I keep forgetting about Adam. That's probably
because you so seldom mention him."

"Not much to say. He's just a kid, though he doesn't realize
that. Sports mad – especially football and athletics. The only
reason he doesn't bunk off school most of the time is because
school is where he can do both things, and he's desperate to get
into the teams. Typical fourteen-year-old – chunkier than
most, quite moody and aggressive at times."

"What has he to be aggressive about?"

"He resents losing his father. He thinks Mum chucked him
out – which she did. They only get to see each other three or
four times a year, which isn't enough for Adam. He wants a
regular dad who comes to watch him every Saturday scoring
goals for the Under-fifteens."

"And Adam was livid about Terry's visit, was he? Why?"

"Well, you can see his point. Suddenly he's got a new big
brother – out of the blue, with no smoothing of the way. Why
was he never told he existed? Why is Mum so delighted he's

turned up again, when she's never been bothered about him before?"

"And why do *you* think that is?"

"I don't know, but I think Adam came close to the mark. When I told him I'd come home and found a young man here, he exploded: he thought it was another of Mum's fancy men. 'I knew it would come to this,' he said. 'She lives in a fantasy world. She'll soon be bringing back *boys* – younger than me.' He gets these ideas about Mother from me, but he does understand them, and he's often right. Anyway, I explained about Terry being her son and our brother."

"How did he take that?"

"I think 'gobsmacked' is the word. He practically choked at the thought. It's the fact that we hadn't been told anything about it. Being told lies is one thing, being told nothing hurts. Somehow Mother is used to having us around, but doesn't care for us, or care about us. It's like we're totally unimportant. It's sort of odd, and rather unpleasant."

"I can imagine."

"Anyway, eventually Adam said: 'I expect she's all over him because he's a new actor in the play called *Peggy*. Someone who'll provide her with all the admiration and adoration we've stopped giving her.'"

"Adam sounds like a sharp young man."

This pulled her up. Then she put aside her reluctance to admit it.

"I suppose he is. Anyway eventually he calmed down, and finally he said: 'She's probably loving all the attention and admiration. It won't last.' And that about sums up Peggy's retreats into a fantasy world: they only last for a short time."

"How do these retreats end?"

"Sometimes in an explosion. More often they get bored, the

men hanging around her. Sometimes she gets bored and goes on to something, or someone else. Mother to a long-lost son is a new and quite a good part, but she hasn't thought twice about him for the first twenty-five years of his life, so I can't see it lasting long."

"That will be hurtful to her son."

"I suppose so. Unless he's playing a part just as much as she is, and moves on quite happily. I'd be more worried about Adam than about Terry."

"About Adam? Why?"

"He's all over the place – emotionally and every other way. He's never really got over the divorce. Sometimes he acts as if he hates Peggy. He'd have gone to live with his father long ago, if his father had been willing to have him. Harry is a traditional soul. He believes children should be looked after by their mothers."

"It must have seemed like rejection."

"Adam tried to tough it out, but I'm sure it did. I heard him crying at night. Harry told him there wasn't room, because he has two young children by his new wife. That didn't make it any better."

They stopped talking as the waiter came along, removed empty dishes, and stocked the table with more. Christa's face lit up with anticipation.

"Can you believe that people used to eat teas like this every day? They must have been enormous! But just for once, it's fantastic!"

She tucked in. Graham was glad she had the elasticity of youth and could slough off melancholy with the arrival of cream sponge and fruit cake. He was glad too that so little eating would be required from himself.

7

En Famille

Whenever the phone rang he hoped it was Christa. He had to restrain himself from running to pick it up. Graham had a keen sense of the ridiculous, particularly where he himself was concerned. Even when he was alone he liked to maintain his dignity.

"Hello?"

"Graham?"

"Yes. Hello Peggy."

He found the voice, now stripped of the distraction of the body, to be like Christa's, but measurably older. Both had an element of flirtation apparently built into them. But Peggy's flirtatiousness reminded him of the past, the briefness of their affair. Christa's seemed like a promise for the future.

"Graham, I want you to do something for me."

"How did you find out my number?" asked Graham, playing for time.

"I looked in Christabel's address book. I knew she had been ringing you."

"Of course. How simple."

The irony and the criticism were quite lost on her.

"Now Graham, don't say no at once," Peggy resumed, the voice becoming almost schoolmistressy. "I'm having a little family reunion – a dinner at Luigi's, my favourite restaurant around here. They worship me there, and they'll do anything for me. It's…it's my birthday, or near enough to it. It's a time for get-togethers and buryings of the hatchet, don't you think? My father and I have had a bit of a difference these last few years – it's really pained me, and he's promised to come. And

Christa and Adam, of course – you'll like Adam. And – well, one or two others. Not actors – they're so competitive, aren't they? But a few relatives and friends – people really close to me. I count you as one of the closest and dearest to me. Will you come, for my sake, and for old time's sake as well?"

Graham's novelist's ear wondered how many times "I", "me" and "my" had figured in the conversation so far. He also noticed the blithe insouciance with which she had changed the story about her parents' deaths.

"I don't know. You haven't given me a date."

"October the first. It was the only date my dad could manage. You remember how close we were in the old days."

Dancing round in the back of his head Graham heard the boast of the young Peggy: "I can twist my dad round my little finger." He refrained from comment on his resurrection from the dead, and gazed down at the empty space under October the first in his desk diary.

"I don't know if I can. There's quite an important engagement that evening. It won't be easy to change it."

"Oh Graham, *please*! For me? Pretty please!"

Graham grimaced into the phone. The awfulness of the appeal made him unwilling to give way at once.

"I'll see what I can do."

"*Please*. Of course you can do it. You're famous."

"I'll give you a ring."

"Oh, you meanie! Do you have my number?"

"Yes. I found it in the telephone directory."

He put down the telephone and thought, going through the conversation step by step. The egotism he could take in his stride. It was not so different from Christa's natural adolescent self-absorption. The thing that surprised him most was the mention of actors. Presumably Peggy still did stage work now and then. Amateur, in all probability. For some reason the fact of her still acting was something he had never till then considered, or asked Christa about. But it was consistent, it made sense: limelight is attractive, even dim, provincial limelight.

The mention of her father he took with a pinch of salt, and he did not believe the dinner was to celebrate a reconciliation with him, or the date fixed with him in mind: elderly widowers were not so busy in the evenings that they only have single isolated free ones. Ted Somers was being hauled in as a make-weight, one of Peggy's few links with the past she shared with Graham.

He had no doubt that the evening was really organised to act out a little drama in which he would play a leading part: his introduction to his son. She was staging a recognition scene straight out of Greek drama or *The Winter's Tale*. He felt he was going to spoil it for her by feeling very little indeed. The truth was, now he had got his thoughts in order, he didn't care whether he met Terry Telford or not. And what did the young man himself feel? He had been keen to meet his mother, that was certain. And that was a feeling many adopted children had. But his father? He didn't seem to have figured very high on Terry's agenda.

He suddenly remembered Peggy mentioning Adam. A reunion between him and Terry could be painful to a boy whose emotional equilibrium had been shattered by the virtual disappearance of his father from his life. He could be shattered by this new encounter. He could turn nasty. Then he wondered whether 'family' could include Adam's father, Peggy's ex. The man who had adopted Christa and then found himself paying maintenance for her. Somehow he didn't see him agreeing to come, or, if he did, fitting in happily or easily with Peggy's plans. He asked Christa about him next time she rang.

"Invited but not coming," she said. "Mum never learns. She thinks everybody loves her and will do whatever she wants. And she had to mention inviting him in front of Adam, with the inevitable disappointment and stormy moods. He was never going to come anyway."

"Why not?"

Christa sighed.

"Mum took him to the cleaners for everything she could get to support us. Or supposedly to support us. Mum enjoys living the high life when she gets the chance, so most of it went on her. My support finished when I was eighteen, but Harry is still stumping up for Adam."

"So he should."

"Agreed. But you can see him being a bit annoyed about me. First she gets him to adopt me, then she throws him out, then she bleeds him dry supposedly to support me."

"I wouldn't be too happy, I admit."

"Are you coming then?"

"I'm tempted," said Graham, reluctance palpable from his voice. "I know perfectly well why the party's being given. I can see that I'm vital to the whole performance."

"Absolutely vital. Are you getting paternal feelings yet?"

"I've just been thinking about that. The answer is a loud no."

"Looks as if the whole thing's going to be a damp squib, then."

"Looks like it. But it's possible Peggy has something unexpected up her sleeve. A *coup de théatre*. By the way, I didn't realize that she still acted."

"Oh yes! Didn't I tell you? She does one big part a year,

though she sometimes does a cameo role as well. The last big one was *Mrs Warren's Profession*."

"Shaw still."

"Prefers Ibsen, struggles with Shakespeare, can't cope with American English, so Tennessee Williams gets mangled."

"Quite a nice little career, though."

"In amateur drama," said Christa, in that voice children throughout the world use about their parents' ambitions. "She still dreams of the head of the National Theatre dropping in on the off-chance to one of her great performances and casting her as Hedda Gabler."

"We all have our dotty dreams," said Graham, whose own was getting an international bestseller. "Well, next time I see you will be at the feast. I suspect I shall feel like Banquo's ghost."

"Oh, *Macbeth*!" said Christa. "We read a bit of that at school."

"Reading a bit of *Macbeth* is a gratuitous piece of literary cannibalism."

"I love it when you use words I don't really understand."

"I don't even think whether you understand them or not."

"That's even better."

He rang Peggy later that day to tell her he would be at the party.

"Oh, you are a dear. Who would have thought all those years ago —"

"I'll be at Luigi's. Seven-thirty all right?"

"Oh, but couldn't you come...Yes. Seven-thirty will be fine."

She had been going to ask him whether he could come to Milton Terrace first, but the thought had struck her that this could have compromised her firm intention to stage a wonderful scene in a public place. Graham told himself that he understood her, knew her through and through. The world revolved around her, and that almighty carousel could be twitched and manipulated to minister to her monstrous sense of self. What didn't happen to her, didn't happen at all *for* her.

He remembered a moment during that meeting at Upper Melrose, the first real meeting they ever had, and the beginning of that very brief affair. He – eighteen, just left school, earnest, convinced they should be talking in depth and with mature seriousness about the play they both had just been in and which had run to great applause – mentioned something in the scene between the Earl of Warwick and Cauchon. "Oh, I wasn't in that bit," Peggy had said. She wasn't in it, so that great scene didn't exist.

He found Luigi's in the Yellow Pages for Romford at the Ipswich Library. He got an odd pleasure from doing such things for himself, without help or advice from his editor or agent or from one of the occasional researchers he had used in the past. Doing it *secretly* was part of the appeal, he admitted to himself. He wanted the relationship with Peggy, her family and friends, to be known only to himself. He drove to London against the early evening rush-hour traffic, and at twenty-past seven was seated at a large table in Luigi's.

"You friend of Mrs Peggy's?" the waiter had said. "Is big celebration. Vonderful lady, Mrs Webster. A real star around 'ere. She love us, an' ve love 'er."

So that was all hunky-dory, thought Graham, studying the menu with half an eye, and the occupied tables with the other half. Mostly Romford, he guessed – couples, or parents with children – with an Italian family by the window (favoured over the loved Mrs Webster, apparently), and a tourist couple, camera on the floor and maps being scanned, at a table over by the wall. Graham was just plumping in his mind for the sea trout (almost certainly farmed in Scotland at some piscine Dotheboys Hall) when an elderly man came into the restaurant. Tired, wary eyes, noted Graham, shoulders bowed, making him look care-worn. A strong man in the past, but now past his best, and without relish for the festivities ahead. When he saw the waiter directing the newcomer to his table, Graham got up."

"I'm Graham Broadbent," he said, holding out his hand.

"I'm Ted Somers," said the man, then frowned. "Graham Broadbent? Then you're —" He stopped, his face now more alive. "Oh dear. Has Peggy got something up her sleeve?"

"Four aces and several jokers I should think."

But they were interrupted. The restaurant's doors on to the street burst open and Peggy sailed in, followed by her party – Christa, a teenage boy, the couple from the greengrocer's and a plump young man, all talking (except the teenage boy) at the tops of their voices. Peggy said "Graham! Dad!" in that order, and rushed over, all billowing voile and matt make-up, embracing Graham as if he'd been her dearest love all her life, instead of for ten days in 1979, then taking her father's hands and giving him a peck on the cheek.

"I know you don't like a fuss, Dad. All that actressy stuff you used to call it. But I *am* an actress, in my little way."

She looked round to try to gather in the plump young man and seat him next to Graham. She mistimed it, however, and Christa who had followed her mother over sank into the seat by Graham, who now found himself between her and her grandfather.

"Have you met Grandad?" Christa asked. "Oh, you have. And this is Adam. We've got to pretend he's drinking lemonade tonight. The Halliburtons you've met, haven't you –

Michael and Vesta. They're both very active with the Romford Players. And this is Terry Telford – you've heard me mention him."

The plump young man nodded, with no particular interest or engagement, and Peggy took charge of him and sat him in the seat nearly opposite Graham, with the Halliburtons beside him. Adam took the lower end of the table, Peggy herself the seat of honour, sitting down grandly as if it was the nearest thing to a throne currently available.

"Well, isn't this nice?" she said, beaming round.

"What are we celebrating?" asked her father.

"Well, my birthday's not far away —" her father frowned, but Peggy studiously refused to notice him – "And I've had a wonderful surprise that I want to share with everyone. Now the first lovely part of any meal: the menu. Don't miss the specials on the board. Luigi's specials are always *very* special! And so are his prosciutto and melons – how he commandeers *all* the just-ripe melons in the country I don't know! No, offence, Michael!" The smiles of the pair from the greengrocer's were a little unripe too. "Now this is Giovanni —" patting a tanned hand to her right, attached to a slim young man with a notebook and a standard waiter's smile – "and he'll take your orders for starters and main course, and then we'll take the sweets as they come."

Ordering broke the ice. Graham stuck with the sea-trout, and had the Stracciatella for first course. He noticed that most of the guests were non-veal-eaters, either for conscientious reasons or because they had never tried it. Christa had spaghetti carbonara and chicken, her brother lasagne and Pizzaiola steak. Adam looked as if he was fuelling rage, and had a glass of red wine in front of him – no pretence of lemonade for him. Ted Somers stuck to minestrone and pork chops, while Peggy chose greedily from the antipasto and ordered duckling for her main course. She was solicitous for the Halliburtons, who opted (except that there was no choice) for the vegetarian main course, preceded by minestrone.

"The vegetarian options really *are* good here," announced Peggy. "Not something just thrown together for cranks."

"We're on the march," observed Vesta. "We're too many to be called cranks. Only a few antediluvian pub landlords regard us as cranks these days."

"I have to keep Michael and Vesta happy," said Peggy. "Not because they're my employers – very good ones they are too – but because Michael has just cast me as Martha in *Who's Afraid of Virginia Woolf?* – something I've yearned to do for years, but was too young. We start rehearsals in a few weeks' time."

There was a little burst of applause in anticipation.

"Pity he doesn't send her to America," whispered Christa to Graham. "Six months and she might get the accent right."

The announcement had caused a little stir of comment and interest at the table, and the American tourists with the camera looked at Peggy curiously, as if they expected to see her name in lights over a West End theatre next time they visited the country. The big table was settling down into little knots of conversation.

"You'll have to excuse me, Mr Broadbent," said Ted Somers. "I was a bit taken aback by your name. A lot of water's flowed under the bridge since then, some of it mucky. Maybe we couldn't have met as friends all those years ago, but we can now. Let bygones be bygones, eh?"

"By all means," said Graham. "I hear you've done pretty well for yourself since moving to Romford."

"Not bad. Better than trying to run a small garage in a small village."

"That's what they say in Bidford."

"Oh, you know the old place, do you? Do you still live in the area?"

"In Suffolk. Hepton Magna, so not all that far away. I was sorry to hear that your wife died recently."

"Aye – it leaves a hole: a big black hole in my case. We'd had a lot of troubles and disappointments in recent years." He threw a glance in the direction of his daughter, one clearly well short of full forgiveness. "Silly of me, but when Mary died I blamed it on the troubles. But it's illnesses that kill you, not sadnesses. Are you married yourself?"

"Separated. I'm not the marrying type. I've learned my lesson."

It was code – a rather dishonest code – for telling Ted he was no longer interested in his daughter. Ted nodded.

"I've got a son too," he said, à propos of nothing. "Steady lad. We never made a lot of him, as we did…you know. But you begin to appreciate the steady type when you get older. He's had his troubles too – beyond what he deserved. But he's straight as a die, is Oliver. I'm grateful for him now."

Talk of sons made Graham conscious that he ought to take some notice of Terry Telford, sitting almost opposite him. The mere thought roused in him feelings of rebellion: he was being manipulated by Peggy, and had come to the "celebration" knowing he would be manipulated. This did not mean he had to offer total co-operation in the process.

He wondered how much Terry Telford knew about the situation. Not very much, he guessed. All would surely have been saved for a big revelation scene. Now he was sitting at Peggy's right hand, getting closer to her than necessary, and putting his hand near hers every time they shared a laugh about something, which was often. Looking at the young man, plump, apparently good-humoured, Graham decided he had a pleasanter impression of the young man than Christa and Adam seemed to have got.

He noticed that Peggy was keeping her eyes, when possible, on the waiters. The first course had been cleared away, and when the main courses began to appear Peggy fingered her glass nervously and kept looking around, up and down "her" table. She's staging Act 1, scene II, Graham thought.

When all the main courses had been delivered, Peggy smiled round at everyone and tapped her glass.

"Now don't stop eating. This is not a toast, yet. I just want to tell you a story, share a piece of news. I told you how Michael had just asked me to play Martha in *Who's Afraid of Virginia Woolf?* I don't know how I'm going to play someone who is so twisted by *not* having children. I've been so blessed in that way – by lovely Christabel and wonderful Adam! Such props and stays for me – and joys too! – they've been always."

Christa smiled coolly, and Adam released not a muscle of his tense, angry face. Graham thought that if he was making the speech he would have seen these as danger signs.

"But one or two of you know of an episode long ago. Something happened to me when I was very young – I strayed from the path, as Graham might put it in one of his lovely novels."

"I'm not Barbara Cartland," protested Graham.

"But you have a heart, Graham, however much you may try to put on this hard cynicism which is fashionable. Anyway, I knew so little then –" (not so ingenue as you're painting yourself, thought Graham) "– and that meant that we moved from our lovely little Essex village to Romford. Believe me, it was something that I've never regretted, thanks to all the lovely, lovely friends I've made here, particularly my *dramatic* friends as I may call them." A special glance was shot at Michael and Vesta. "But the early heartbreak was that I had to give up the baby that I bore – such a love! So small and helpless! Things were different then, you know, and there were pressures…"

"There were no pressures from us," muttered Ted Somers.

"I'm not accusing anyone, Dad…So all my life I've carried around in me this heartbreak, this something that I've had and then lost, and thought I could never find again. Perhaps this heartbreak has added something to my performances on stage – it's not for me to say…Anyway, it just shows how one has to have faith. Because one day, three weeks ago – September the tenth it was, and I'll never forget the date – I had a phone-call, and there was something in the voice and I *knew* from the moment I heard it that this was one of the most important phone-calls of my life: He asked me if I had been Peggy Somers, and —" she smiled roguishly – "to cut a long story not very short, he announced that he was the child I'd given up for adoption all those weary years ago, when I was eighteen. Christa and Adam have met him, we all love him already, and I wanted to introduce him to all my family and friends, so we can all be open about it, all welcome him."

She stood up, looked around at them all, and raised her glass.

"To Terry Telford, my son."

Not just an echoing of the sentiments but applause seemed to be called for, and that presented problems. Who was to be applauded, and what for? Graham tried to solve the matter when he put down his glass, having sipped, and extended his hand over the table, saying "Welcome". Michael and Vesta followed his example and so, after a moment's hesitation, did Ted Somers.

"I suppose I'm your grandfather," he said. "Welcome."

Graham was beginning to wonder, with dread, when all this loving was going to lead to the inevitable revelation. He looked at Peggy, but all she did was respond with an enigmatic smile. He felt he was only ministering to her self-absorption, and he looked away in disgust. As he did so his eye rested on the other end of the table. Adam was sitting there, his face twisting with real fury – genuine feeling, as opposed to all the actressy falseness emanating from Peggy and from her new-found son, who was again caressing her hand on the table and looking into her eyes, while both were masticating their main courses. Graham felt the intensity of Adam's feelings was a relief, but he had to recognise that it was a threat as well. He had helped to initiate a train of events that could end in catastrophe for Peggy and her fragile family.

"So that," came Peggy's voice, resuming the play, "is how I come to know my first-born, the son I'd had and never had. And what it proves to me is that happy endings do happen. 'Sometimes – there's God – so quickly!' as Blanche DuBois says." If Graham had not noticed the rotten Southern accent Christa's nudge would have told him. "And from now on, Terry and I are going to make up for all that wasted time. I'll never be alone again."

"Alone?" Adam's voice came from the end of the table, breaking in anger or contempt. "You'll never be *alone* again? Haven't Christa and I been anyone? Have we just been inconvenient nothings who should never have intruded into your life?"

Peggy's hand went to her mouth.

"Adam! Darling, you're misunderstanding. I never meant —"

"Oh, you meant what you said, *Mother*! All we've been to you is walking maintenance payments. I'm sick of you. I'm sick of living with you, having you near me. I'd rather sleep on the streets and beg. I'd rather sell myself. I'd rather be dead."

He kicked back his chair and ran from the restaurant, withholding his tears till he was outside and the door well shut, but then breaking out as if his heart was broken. The restaurant had fallen very silent in the last minute or two, and the tears penetrated inside.

"Oh, the silly boy," said Peggy. "Don't let him spoil our evening. He's still only a child, and he's not used to the idea of his new, wonderful brother."

"Someone should go to him," Graham whispered to Ted and Christa.

"His sister would be best," said Ted. "I'm afraid I've never really understood the boy."

"I'll go," said Christa, wiping her mouth. "I'll give him a minute or two and then I'll go."

"Tell him living on the streets is out of the question," said Graham. "He can bunk down at my house while he sorts himself out. Christa, you both can, at any time. You must remember that."

Christa nodded and smiled absently, as if the offer had always been assumed by her. The waiters, possibly with earlier experience of Peggy's celebrations going awry, had hurried the sweets trolley away from a distant table and began a gabble through the alternatives to cover the awkwardness, which in any case was apparently not perceptible to Peggy, who was giggling with Terry in a way that could only be described as flirtatious.

"I'll have the strawberry shortcake, or the Tiramisu – whatever," said Christa, and slipped away from the table and out through the door to the street. This left Graham feeling still more marooned in company that was indifferent or positively hostile to him. And with a public revelation by Peggy, delivered in the most cringe-making style and English, still in prospect.

Peggy had chosen a concoction which was mostly artificial cream, and the plate looked as if all the ingredients had been delivered by cannon. Terry was looking at it and laughing, and Peggy, still in a giggly mood, was forcing a piled-up spoonful into his mouth. Graham was possessed of an almost irresistible urge to push back his chair and go out to join the hunt for Adam, who suddenly seemed to him the most appealing person at the table, because he was possessed of real emotion.

Peggy, however, self-regarding as she generally was, had a sympathetic understanding when confronted by an emotion which related to herself. She sensed what Graham, hardly seen for twenty-five years, felt about the scene that was being enacted. She tore herself from Terry's seduction of her and fixed Graham with a smile that was not in any way come-hither. Indeed, it was almost basilisk, paralysing his will.

"There's one more thing," she said.

The table went quiet. Had they all been expecting this? All eyes were on Peggy, but Graham somehow got the impression that the Halliburtons were trying desperately not to look at him. Egotism, he told himself.

"*Just* one more, then Peggy will shut up and let you all relax and enjoy yourselves. You know how honoured we all feel that we have with us tonight Graham Broadbent, one of the most talented of that wonderful generation of English novelists that emerged in the Eighties and Nineties." Of whom Peggy, Graham suspected, could have named no other. "Graham and I go way back, he to his last year in Grammar School, me to my last months living in those parts – living with my dear old dad here, and Mum who's no longer with us. We met in a school play – my first starring role – but we *really* met a few weeks later, in a churchyard. Graham was wondering whether to go to London University, and I was expecting to do my last year at school, and perhaps be in another play with Colchester Grammar Boys. And we met. It wasn't love at first sight, or anything like that, but it was attraction, and I *know* I suspected then what a distinguished figure Graham was to become."

"I was just a snotty-nosed schoolboy," said Graham, with that false self-deprecation that gushing speeches often elicit from their victims.

"If you had been a snotty-nosed schoolboy, I wouldn't have been interested, darling," said Peggy. "And I definitely was interested. What we had was short, but it was very beautiful. We weren't children, but we were young: we were starry-eyed, impulsive, and ill-prepared." There was a little laugh, Graham thought from Vesta Halliburton. "I am sometimes surprised by how often girls get caught out these days, after all the education, and all the awful warnings in the soaps, but still they do. We – genuinely – knew nothing. Soon after the lovely, brief romance was over, I found I was pregnant. And I think all of you bright, intelligent people will have guessed what I am going to say. It seems like magic – the best – most lovely sort of magic. Suddenly my Terry here has not only a new mum, but a new dad."

Graham had been transfixed by Peggy, by the awfulness of the speech, and dread of what was coming. Now he looked at Terry – something Peggy had not done during the entire speech. Terry's face was fixed on her, but imprinted on it was not joy or euphoric surprise. It was stupefaction, disgust, revulsion. Was it real emotion? Graham wondered. Or acting? Terry was after all Peggy's son. "Yes, the boy I had by that unexpected pregnancy was Terry, and Terry's natural father is, happily, with us tonight. It's a wonderful feeling at last to reunite father and son."

There was a clatter. Terry had stood up with a vengeance, his chair flying behind him. The American tourists, perhaps thinking this was a rehearsal for a play, or perhaps that this was a family row involving one of Britain's foremost actresses, were taking snaps. Terry's face was certainly a picture – beetroot with rage.

"What is this crap? You're talking fucking nonsense – taking me for a fool. This man's not my natural father. I don't need a natural father. I know my natural father already."

8

Into Thin Air

For the second time that evening an exit was made.

Like the first one it was the exit of a pride-injured male, and it therefore had a similarity – it seemed to the watchers in the nature of a replay. What was quite different was Peggy's reaction to it. She gazed at the door shutting behind Terry, and then looked distractedly round, first at one face, then at another, then to her various 'things' – handbag, purse, make-up bag on the table around her, then to her coat hanging on a stand by the door.

"I must go after him," she said, seeming worried and upset. She gathered up the various receptacles, then put them back in a heap while she fetched her coat and put it over all the billowing voile. It was a light coat, in an interesting green, and it suited her. She knew it, and she posed while she looked round to see if there was anything she had forgotten.

"Adam didn't get this kind of concern from her," whispered Graham to Ted Somers.

"And he's only fourteen," said Ted. They watched as Peggy, without goodbyes, sailed out of Luigi's and into the night.

"I think we'd better go after them," said Graham. "Have you got your car?"

"Yes. I'm an old garage man, remember. Driving skills are the last things to go."

"It seems like overkill: two perfectly capable young males. Still, Adam at least is still very much under age."

"It's only Adam I'm worrying about. And Christa."

"Me too. A twenty-five-year-old male should be perfectly safe in Romford on a Monday night. Still, it seems to be Terry that Peggy is looking for. We've got four people looking for two. Surely one of us must strike lucky."

"You'd think so. But I'm not sure my eyesight's up to recognising this new one."

Graham took 'this new one' to be Terry Telford, and refrained from wondering whether Ted should be driving. They got themselves together and were starting for the door when they were confronted by Luigi and a large waiter who looked as if he originated from the North of Luigi's country – wide, hard-faced and determined. It was Luigi who was brandishing a piece of paper.

"The bill, gen'lemen. The bill."

Graham and Ted looked at each other.

"But Mrs Webster —" Graham began.

"Oh no, sir. This 'as 'appened before. You are friends and family. You 'ave good chance of getting the money. I – never!"

Ted and Graham looked at each other. Then they burst out laughing.

"Landed in it again!" said Ted. "At my age too. Only proves there's no fool like an old fool."

They halved the bill, paid it – Ted with cash, Graham with credit card – and then they both went out into the night. A light drizzle was beginning to fall.

"We'd better keep in touch," said Graham. "Have you got your mobile with you?"

"No. I stick to the law about not using a mobile: it's a sensible one. But I'll go back home periodically, in case Adam's there. It's 88 Silverdale Street. You can leave a note."

"And I expect I'll come back here now and then. Both the lads were a bit hasty – annoying though Peggy is. They could have second thoughts and return to base, thinking we could still be eating."

They separated, Graham noting that Ted had an old Jaguar, Ted noting that Graham had a newish Honda Civic. The other big difference between them, Graham decided as he set off, was that Ted knew the roads he was driving, where he did not. He could only cruise around the centre and near-centre of Romford, registering the odd place he already recognised – the Jeremy Bentham College, Milton Terrace (number twenty-five was shrouded in darkness), the Halliburtons' shop, and Luigi's, still busy and throbbing. He looked at the occasional body wrapped in blankets huddled in shop or office doorways. Surely Adam couldn't be so well-prepared as to be already equipped for sleeping rough? On the other hand if he had been home there was no reason why he shouldn't have grabbed a couple of blankets from a drawer and be getting what sleep he could in an unusual and frightening situation.

Now and again there was a half-hearted shower of rain. It was not cold, and there was no reason in the weather why a healthy fourteen-year-old shouldn't fare perfectly well during a night in the open. No reason in most weathers – there was the rub. The dangers came from people. A mixed-up adolescent, picked up by a paedophile or some still more dangerous kind of weirdo – the idea didn't bear thinking of.

Now and then in his cruising he raised a hand to Ted Somers doing likewise. Eventually, three quarters of an hour into his search, he spotted Christa. He pulled into the kerb beside her, glad to have found someone he knew, and who knew the area.

"No luck?" he asked. She shook her head miserably.

"Why don't you jump in? I'd be more effective with someone who knows him well, and you'd cover more ground."

She thought for a moment, then hopped into the passenger seat.

"Any theories, any idea what to do next?" Graham asked.

"Not really. I thought about going to look at one or two of the people sleeping rough —"

"Risky. You'd very much better not try that. I thought about it, but cried off."

"Oh, it wouldn't worry me," said Christa airily, as if buxom young women ran no risks in a modern town. "But I just couldn't imagine Adam sleeping in a doorway. He thinks of himself as a hard man, but really he likes his creature comforts. Anyway, I thought I'd only do it if I recognised the blankets."

"I suppose that makes sense. I've been past your house. It's in darkness. I suppose it's not inconceivable that Adam has simply gone home and gone to bed."

"Pride would stop him, I reckon," said Christa. "But we could go home and see if there's any sign of either of them."

"Either of them? Did Terry have a key to your house?"

"Not that I know of, but he could have. But why would he go there if he's pissed off with Mum? I saw Grandad and he told me what happened. He was back at his house, checking up there. I should think Terry just caught the first train home. No, I meant Adam and Mother. If she's out looking for Terry I can't understand why I haven't caught sight of her."

"Right, then let's go to Milton Terrace. Direct me."

It turned out to be an easy journey – a right turn, five minutes straight drive, then a turn-off from just above Halliburtons' greengrocery shop into the maze of between-the-war semis. When Graham pulled up outside number twenty-five he was frowning.

"Isn't that a light – a dim one?"

"Yes. I think it could be the light in the big cupboard-like thing Peggy had built in the hall for coats and macs and boots and Adam's sports things. She was going with a builder at the time."

"Well, I think someone must have been back."

"Maybe Mother came home for a warmer coat than the one she wore to Luigi's. It's a favourite with her, but it's really a summer coat. Or maybe Adam came for some of his sports things."

"What on earth could he want with them?"

"Maybe he couldn't bear to leave them behind. Qualifying for the Under-fifteens would win out over rage at Mum any day. It's sort of Linus's blanket with him. I can imagine him sleeping rough with his football boots for comfort."

"Come on. Let's go and have a look."

Christa let them in, and put the light on. The hall had been a good-sized one, but the cupboard to the right of the door cut down the space. The door was open and Christa looked in.

"Looks like I was wrong about Adam's sports things. They all seem to be here."

"We could check upstairs. He could be in bed."

"Maybe…Mother's coat she wore to Luigi's is here, and a thicker one has gone…And a pair of walking shoes. She wore high-heels to Luigi's, because the Halliburtons took us in their car."

"The changes make sense if she was going to tramp the streets looking for Adam or Terry."

Christa screwed up her forehead.

"Yes, apart from the fact that neither of us saw her doing any tramping." She cast her eye around the hall, but saw nothing out of place. "Let's just have a look in the front room." She opened the door and switched on the light. "Ah."

A dining table dominated the room. On the table was a sheet of exercise book paper, lined, and torn from its binder.

They both went over and leant over it to read, Graham very conscious of the closeness of the girl. The note was in fact two notes, in different handwritings. The top one was in a childish hand that was just beginning to find individual characteristics of its own.

> Im leaving mum. Im fed up with being the one who you love only when your trying to make an effect. You don't care a bit about me or Christa or anyone except yourself. Id rather be on my one, don't look for me.

The other handwriting was undoubtedly adult, but with little flourishes and curlicues for effect.

> I don't give a naughty word whether you go or stay, but I'm willing to bet you'll be here when I come back. I'm going off with a friend for a few days. Any problems Christa, go to Michael and Vesta — or Graham might like to give a hand. About bleeding time I'd say.

"Sorry about that," said Christa, embarrassed.

"Don't worry. Since I was never told about Terry there wasn't much I could do." He thought for a moment. "I wonder what I would have done if I had been told."

"Anything but marry her. We mustn't show Adam this."

"You mean he'll see it as some kind of challenge, and it'll make him still more determined to stay away?"

"Yes…I wonder if he's gone to Mickey Leatherby's."

"Who's that? One of his friends?"

"Adam just has chums — mates he hangs about with but never really confides in. But Mickey's the one he's closest to. They share a mania for football — athletics too, but not so passionately."

"Where does Mickey live?"

"I think it's Hamnet Street. I'll look him up."

Hamnet Street it was, number forty-eight. Since it sounded as if this was the only "friend" Adam would have thought of going to, Graham agreed it was worth a try. Christa said it was a ten minutes' drive away, and after a quick trip upstairs to check on Adam's bedroom, which was empty and undisturbed, they went out to the car again and Christa gave directions in intervals of talking.

"We left the light on in the hall cupboard," she said, as they drove away.

"I know. I thought about it, but decided we should leave things as they were when we arrived."

She shot him a glance.

"Why?"

"In case we have to call in the police."

"Why would we?"

"Christa, women who go away leaving their children (sorry, one of their children) to fend for themselves, and any woman who disappears with 'a friend', are possible objects for the police to investigate. At some point we may have to decide among ourselves whether to call them in."

Christa considered this.

"But she's done it before, more than once."

"That makes it worse. What did you do? Just cope until she came back?"

"Yes. I can look after Adam. We got on all right."

"I'm sure you did, but that's not the point. And this time there's the complicating factor that Adam had decided to leave home, and announced it in his mother's presence."

"Will the police take that seriously?"

"I don't know. We all did, didn't we? And the police won't

think much of a mother who takes off just when her fourteeen-year-old son has run away – and who leaves a note that says in effect that she doesn't give a damn."

Christa pondered this.

"You don't like Mum much, do you?"

"No. I thought I might when I met her again, but no: I don't like her, and I don't think much of her either."

"This is Hamnet Street. Go slow – it's difficult to see the numbers…That was thirty-six…This is forty. We're going in the right direction…This must be forty-eight."

Graham stopped the car. The house was a detached one from the same era as the Milton Terrace house, and thousands more all over Romford. The hedges were low and well-cared-for, and they gave a view of the whole house. One room had lights on that blazed through their flimsy curtains.

"They're still up," said Christa.

"It could be a family conference. There are no lights on anywhere else – kitchen or bedrooms for example. We'd better think about whether we should interrupt it. If it's a conference about Adam we might annoy him, especially if he thought they were about to let him stay. We could ruin our chances of influencing him."

"Maybe I should go on my own —" Christa began.

"I was about to suggest that," said Graham, grateful again for her fund of common sense. "I'm an unknown quantity to Adam, and there's no reason why he should like or trust me."

"He and I have always been good mates. We get on, because we have to. I think it would be best if I went on my own. I could feel a fool, of course: we don't know yet whether he's actually here."

But they soon did. They were interrupted by the front door

opening. Two shadowy figures were just visible in the hall, but through the door came Adam, his school bag on his back, walking with a hang-dog slump to his shoulders. The fire of his departure from Luigi's was now burning very low. Christa's face twisted with pity. She wound down the window and called his name softly as he came out through the gate on to the street.

"Adam."

He jumped, looked as if he might run, then saw her face.

"Did they chuck you out?" Christa asked.

"Yes. They wouldn't even let me stay overnight – just said I ought to go home and make it up with Mother."

"You'd have a job. She's gone off again."

"With a man?"

"What do you think? She left a note…Why don't you get into the car?"

Adam, without reluctance, got in. His relief was palpable, but so was his sheepishness. Christa slipped out of the car and got into the back seat with him.

"I'm sorry I jumped," Adam muttered. "You get strange ideas…"

"I'm sure you do," said Graham. "It seems so easy, living rough, when you think about it, but it's hard and dangerous when you try it."

"Yeah…But I don't know what to do. I mean, even if Mum's not there going home seems —"

"A bit of a climb down. Yes. Anyway, I'm not sure it's a good idea. Your mother comes home, there you both are all safe and she gets the idea that taking off is somewhat *all right*…And in my book it isn't. There's your grandfather."

Christa made a face.

"He'd cope for a few days, but he wouldn't like it. He's not great with people our age. If Kath was there, it would be better —"

"Kath from Bidford?"

"That's right. They get on really well together. There's Grandma Webster in Stanway, but it's a bit the same there: we love her, and she loves us coming on a visit, but anything more than a few hours she's not too happy about."

"Look," said Graham, starting the car. "We shouldn't be discussing this, late at night on a drizzly street after a difficult evening. I live an hour away, Adam. I've got a guest bedroom and a little box of a room. Will you both come back with me, for a night or two at least? So we can discuss what should happen next, without any pressure?"

"Yes," said Adam, trying to keep the extent of his relief out of his voice. But he added: "It's very kind of you."

"Not at all. Peggy seemed to think that because I had nothing to do with Terry I was a bit responsible for you two."

"That's just garbage," said Adam bitterly. "Peggy's garbage. The sort of thing she thinks up to get people to do the things she ought to be doing herself."

"I rather think you're right," said Graham. "Especially as Peggy didn't have a lot to do with Terry's upbringing herself. So regard this as just a lonely middle-aged author getting himself a bit of companionship for a while, between books."

"I'd better ring Grandad," said Christa, taking out her mobile. She pressed numbers expertly in the near-darkness, then said: "He's on 'Answer'. He almost never does that. He must have put it on when he went back home, to keep in touch tonight…Grandad, we've found Adam. He's fine. We're all going down to Hepton Magna, to stay with Graham for the night. Love you." She put her mobile away. "I bet he's relieved."

They were beginning to leave the hideous parts of Essex that were no more than London suburbs. Graham could see in his mirror that in the back seat Adam's head was resting on Christa's shoulder, his eyes shut. It was ten minutes later, when he saw Adam waking up and blinking, that he said:

"It doesn't have to be just a night at my place, you know. We ought to sit down tomorrow and decide exactly what is best for *you two.*"

Christa thought about this.

"You think it might be a good idea for us to get away from Romford for a bit, don't you?"

"Yes. Maybe."

"That means get away from Mum."

"Well…I shouldn't judge her…I don't think your mother behaved very well tonight. I don't think she put your interests first."

There was a duet of chortles and snorts from the back.

"You don't have to be embarrassed about criticising Mum," said Christa. "Our family is not a mother and two children, it's three independent people. Mother has *never* put our interests first, so we don't owe her, and certainly don't give her, any particular respect as a parent."

"I see…I do feel in a way that she should be taught not to take you for granted – that she can't just come back and you children would move back in and everything would revert to normal."

"Teach her a lesson, you mean?"

"In a way, yes."

"She'd think all her birthdays had come at once." There was now an outright burst of laughter from the back. "She's wanted to get rid of us for years, you know. It would give her her 'freedom'. She's happy with Terry because he doesn't threaten her freedom in any way."

"Not that we stop her doing anything much," said Adam.

"You're probably right," said Graham. "But that shouldn't stop us doing anything if that thing is the best for *you*. I think it would be advisable to try to find a school for Adam – just temporarily. It would make it clear that he does have other choices, and it would look good if the authorities start sticking their noses in. And then there's you, Christa, and your courses at the Jeremy Bentham College."

"They're pretty understanding there, especially about difficult home conditions. If you could get me to a railway station I could stay the night in Romford when I need to, otherwise work from home. Your home. I'll need to collect books and clothes and things from Milton Terrace."

"These are all just possibilities, of course," said Graham. "What do you say, Adam?"

"I don't know…It's very nice of you…but I was hoping to get selected for the Under-fifteens."

"This is a lot more important than the Under-fifteens," said Christa tartly.

Graham rushed in with balm.

"Romford is a place with a big catchment area. I'm not an expert, but I should have thought if you're considered promising in a Romford school, you'll be considered bloody brilliant in any school you might go to in my part of the world."

"Oh? I hadn't thought of that," said Adam.

Ten minutes later he said:

"It would have to be a football school. I wouldn't go to a rugger school."

"Of course," said Graham with a straight face.

Never underestimate the elasticity of youth, he said to himself. Whenever, as he covered the journey to home, he could see Adam's face in the mirror he was looking out of a window, his eyes bright. Once he even saw a smile on his face.

9

The Morning After

They got to bed very late that Monday night. Graham tried to be businesslike, and organised the two beds very efficiently, but of course the two children (I must stop thinking of them *both* as children, Graham had said to himself) were stimulated by the new surroundings, their sudden change of circumstances: even after they had all gone to bed Graham heard them talking in the tiny extra bedroom which Christa had taken, on the grounds that she would only be around in Hepton Magna for part of the time, so Adam should have the guest room. It was around two when Graham finally dropped off to sleep, and he rather thought next morning that they were still talking then.

When he awoke at nine-fifteen he listened. They *were* still talking, or rather talking again, downstairs. Probably they'd rummaged around to get themselves breakfast. He took advantage of their preoccupation to use for the first time the telephone he'd had installed in his bedroom after his wife had left him. The person he rang was the headmistress of the local secondary school – a woman he knew well enough to exchange casual social banalities with. He explained to her Adam's current predicament.

"So his mother has gone off without making adequate provision for the children?" Mrs Hayward asked.

"Without making any provision. One of the 'children' is nineteen – the age, I suppose, when they're delighted to be left on their own."

"That doesn't mean they should be, or that they should be left in charge of a younger sibling."

"Adam is fourteen, sports mad, and inclined to bunk off school, except that he's scared of not being selected for the various elevens, squads or whatever. The bunking-off is something, I suspect, that Peggy, his mother, can take in her stride – pay no attention to, in fact – but I feel he should get some schooling as long as she is away."

"Of course. And you've no idea how long that will be?"

"No. It's not as though she's gone on a package holiday. She's just gone off with a man, identity unknown."

"I see. It sounds a very unsatisfactory situation. Well, we'll do what we can for the boy."

"I'll bring him along when they've finished breakfast, if that's all right by you."

"Can I suggest that you *send* him along? Hepton Magna is not a large place so he can't miss the school. Coming on the first day with a parent, or someone in loco parentis, can arouse ridicule when you're a fourteen-year-old. The third year have sports on Tuesday afternoons, so that will be a good time for Adam to make his own way."

"Excellent idea. Many thanks."

Adam showed something of a child's traditional reluctance to go to a new school, but the idea of being a large fish in a small pond won out, and he went off reasonably happily, even agreeing to take one of Graham's blank exercise books (in which he first-drafted his novels) as a token that he might do some regular school work.

"So what will you do?" Graham asked Christa when Adam had set off, both of them still chewing toast at the table.

"I think I should go and collect more clothes and books, and let them know at the college that things are going to be a bit haywire in the near future. I can stay the night with my friend Josie rather than alone at home, then I can go to a lecture or two, come back tomorrow evening, and stay till Monday. I think Adam will settle in better with me around."

"I think so too," said Graham heartfeltly. "So what we do next is get you to a station."

Two hours later, with Christa seen off to London from Ipswich station, Graham was home and waiting for Adam to return from school. He decided to fill in the time by informing anyone who would be interested what the situation of Peggy's two children was. The first person had to be Peggy's father. Ted was glad to hear from him, but he himself had no fresh news.

"Nothing at all, I'm afraid," he said. "I kept looking till two thirty, but then I went to bed. I'd got your message about Adam and Christa. Christa can take care of herself, so Adam is the main one I worry about. I can't care any longer about Peggy. What can be done about a middle-aged woman who's man-mad and lives in a fantasy world?"

"I don't know," said Graham. "I *am* worried about her, and that's the truth. She's gone off with a 'friend'. OK, probably a man. But what kind of man friend? An instant one, made on the street? More likely someone she knows a bit but not well. Going off with a man can be dangerous rather than pleasant. It's the sort of thing any parent warns a teenage girl against. I think the police should be brought in on this."

"Oh Lord," said Ted. "That means you want me to do it, doesn't it?"

"I'd be grateful if you would."

"I will, I suppose, but I feel quite embarrassed doing it. How do I explain if, after ten years of having nothing to do with my daughter, I call in the police when she's only been gone a night? And claims to be with a friend?"

"They'll understand it's basically a formality. You're not exactly calling them in to search for her. The important thing is that they are notified that none of her family knows where she is, and they have a description of her on their files."

"In case a body is found," said Ted unhappily.

"Well yes, that, but only among other possibilities."

"Oh Lord."

Adam came back some time after four. Graham watched him walking from the direction of the school. He had a boy of his own age on either side of him, and they were talking and laughing. Graham realised at once that the day had been a great success, and that his first major decision on Adam, to get him a temporary placing in school, had been the right one.

When he came in Adam was full of his day, the game of soccer he'd played that afternoon – in which he'd shone, in his own eyes at least – and the boys he'd palled up with.

"Oh, and I had school dinner, is that all right?"

"It's fine. What about lessons?"

Adam went vague on those, but at least it was clear that he'd been to some.

"Oh, and I'm going to Jack's place later on to download some tracks."

"That's OK. When would you like to eat?"

"I told you, I had school dinner."

"Well, have a sandwich. I don't want you begging Jack's mother for food."

Adam seemed to have undergone a metamorphosis. From the glowering figure with the outsize chip on his shoulder he had become a contented (and rather full-of-himself) fourteen-year-old. He wolfed down two ham sandwiches, had a shower (because the showers at school were 'really primitive') and breezed out of the house. Graham noted the shower: Adam was obviously a boy who had never had maternal scoldings about keeping clean. But being a sportsman he had worked out a regime for himself.

The evening stretched out, but then it always had. He hadn't noticed it when he was on his own. He didn't fancy music, or the television rubbish he often indulged in (television was the right medium for rubbish, he contended, and it did it much better than it did the serious stuff). There remained the entertainment medium which he realized he had become rather addicted to in the past few weeks: the telephone. He rang Enquiries, with nothing beyond the surname Telford and the place Wimbledon. He got two names, with the initials D and S. He rang the second.

"2789641."

"Is that Mrs Telford?"

"No, it's Miss or Ms, whichever you prefer. I'm not bothered. I'm Sarah Telford."

"Ah, I think I've got the wrong number. I was wanting to speak to the parents of Terry Telford."

"Oh, that's my mum and dad. The number's in the directory, and it's D for Derek."

"I've got it then. I wonder if you could help me, though, and then I wouldn't have to bother them. It's a slightly delicate matter, potentially."

"I'll try, of course."

Graham swung into fictional mode.

"I'm a journalist, and I'm doing an article – it may develop into a series – on people who have been adopted and have sought out their birth parents."

"I feel I've seen articles on that subject before."

Sharp, Graham thought. Be careful.

"There's nothing new under the sun, especially in journalism," he said, sounding confident. "Now Terry is adopted, isn't he?"

"That's right."

"And he's discovered both his birth father and mother."

There was a definite silence.

"It's news to me if he has," she said at last.

"That was what I was told. Does this mean that his adoptive parents have been kept in the dark about this?"

"Well if they knew, I'm quite sure I would have been told."

"You're in regular touch with them?"

"I was round there this morning, and Terry rang while I was there. We talked afterwards about him doing supply teaching, and hoping to get a permanent teaching position. Nothing at all was said about his birth parents. My mum and dad have never said anything about it. It hasn't been discussed as far as I know."

"Nothing? Ever?"

"Perhaps I shouldn't have said 'never'. They may have said – speculated, as it were – that one day he might want to find out who his mother was, maybe make contact with her. Nothing more than that."

"Do you think your parents would be upset if he did that?"

There was another pause.

"I honestly don't know. I should think they'd prefer it if they were told first. It's possible that they might feel it as a kind of blow, a comment on them as parents. Though God knows Terry got more love than any child I know."

"Were you adopted too?"

"No. But it was a difficult birth, and Mum was told not to have any more. I was ten when Terry arrived, so he got an awful lot of love from me as well. How did you know – if it's true – that Terry had met up with his birth parents?"

Graham once again drew on his talents as a fiction writer.

"I was with a crowd at a club. He was one of them – I've seen him but not spoken to him. It was mentioned that he'd sought out his birth parents, and was very happy with both of them. That's why he seemed to be an ideal subject. But the adoptive parents are very much in the picture as far as my article is concerned, and of course I couldn't approach them if Terry himself hasn't."

"I'm quite sure he hasn't."

"It seems an odd situation: his friends know he's done this, but his parents don't."

The definite, decided voice at the other end came straight back.

"It doesn't seem odd to me at all. When you were in your teens and twenties I bet you had a lot of things in your life that your friends knew about, but which you made damned sure your parents didn't."

"Point taken. I don't think your parents are going to be suitable for my piece, especially as I wouldn't want to upset them. Would you keep quiet about this call?"

"Of course. They're very gentle people. I'd hate to upset them."

Putting the phone down, Graham had again a vision of his mother, hair covered by a knotted headscarf, her hands plunged into hot washing-up water in the sink. The image was succeeded by another: of his mother at school sports day, at which he never shone and only tried to mark time convincingly. But her face was bright with pride – perhaps at how convincingly he was faking, perhaps because she was taken in herself.

That image in its turn was succeeded by another: of his father in the garden, where he worked all the hours he could secure from his spare time. He could not understand why

Graham would not join him, and why he sometimes made remarks like: "There's more to life than working in the garden."

"There is," he would say. "But nothing that gives half the satisfaction."

Yes, there had been things in his young life that he had never shared with his parents. Then he remembered that he had never said anything about Peggy to any of his friends either.

Adam got back quite early from Jack's. He said he'd had a good time, but it was obvious he could hardly keep his eyes open. The events of Monday night were taking their toll. He went off to bed, and Graham missed his company. But he missed that of Christa still more.

She returned the next evening. She had put in a few appearances at classes and lectures, but she had made her position clear to the principal. She had been home to Milton Terrace, accompanied by her friend Josie (she couldn't explain why she was nervous, but she was, and got out of the house as quickly as possible). She had piled clothes and books into the largest suitcase she could find, then made sure Graham met her at Ipswich station. His heart leapt within him when he saw how long-term she apparently regarded her stay with him as being.

"Won't Darren miss you?" he asked, gesturing at the case.

"Who?"

"Isn't that your boyfriend's name?"

"Oh, *Dar*ren! I'd forgotten him. I haven't seen him for *ages*."

"Can't be much more than ten days," said Graham. "You mentioned him in Green Park."

"It seems like ages, so much has been going on. I'm single and looking at the moment."

Graham felt quietly pleased. He couldn't think of any young

man in Hepton Magna who would fit the bill for a sophisticated young Romfordian.

"How are things at home?" he asked.

"Same as when we were there. I left a note on the table so she knows where we are when she eventually comes home."

"That was sensible. You didn't go to the police?"

"Oh no. Grandad says he's told them she's gone missing, and I don't see they need to know any more than that. The less they start bothering themselves with Adam and me the better."

That was a sentiment Graham could only agree with.

For the rest of the week Christa went about the business of settling in. She took over the cooking, which was mainly for her and Graham, since Adam preferred lunch at school, which left him free (if occasionally hungry) in the evenings. He opted to spend his evenings with his growing circle of friends, which Graham had to tell himself was absolutely normal. Christa began the same process of finding a circle of young people of her own age, and on Friday evening went into Bury St Edmunds with them, describing it as Dullsville, but quite pleasant. Unspoken between her and Graham was the fact that Peggy had not rung. One day when Christa was out he rang Mrs Poulson, the next-door neighbour he had spoken to on his first visit to the Webster house. She said there was no sign of life in the house, beyond the fact that Christa had come and gone. He phoned the Halliburtons as well, and they said there had been no sign of Peggy at the shop. They didn't think there was any need to worry.

On Sunday he took Christa and Adam to visit their grandmother in Stanway, making sure they rang her first to assure her they weren't being dumped on her, and would just be with her for a couple of hours or so.

"That was sensible," said Christa in the car. "I don't know

why she thinks she's going to be landed with us for life, but she does."

"Grandparents are the new exploited class," said Graham. "Their children go out to work, both parents, and they dump their littlies on the oldies without even having the decency to pay them."

"It's not as though she would have to wheel me round all day in a pram," said Adam.

"True. But she probably realizes that it's when children become teenagers that the problems start," said Graham.

"I don't know why you should say that. I've been no trouble. You don't know what problems are *yet*."

They all laughed, but Graham was conscious that Adam's remarks were both good-natured and true.

Mrs Webster was the perfect stage granny from the neck up, but she was clad in track-suit bottoms and trainers lower down, and as she said with a wry smile: "I'm damned if I was going to put on Sunday best for you lot." She'd put together a table of cold meats and salads in the two hours since they had rung, and she had also had the foresight to forget about 'afters' so that she could send the 'children' on the ten minute walk to the nearest supermarket. Graham knew she wanted to talk, and, watched by three censorious cats, he gave her a succinct account of the events of the past week.

"It's all in character," she said when he had finished. "Peggy always did exactly as she pleased, all the time she was married to my son Harry. No other consideration entered into it."

"I gather she even swindled her father out of the house."

"That's right. She got it for a song simply by refusing to pay the rest she was owing. Though she paid in a way. It was the last straw for my Harry: he'd winked at all sorts of behaviour – moral, legal, sexual behaviour that was way over the limits.

But he drew the line on her cheating her dad. There was no way he could pay off what was owing, so he just took off."

"When was this?"

"About ten years ago, just after they moved to Milton Terrace. Christa was old enough to understand something of what happened."

"And now Harry is married again, I believe?"

"Yes, he is. You're thinking of Adam, I suppose – I know how upset he is about losing contact. I'm afraid Harry is the type who makes one bad choice after another. His wife seems to make him happy, but it's by keeping him completely under her thumb. There's no way she's going to take responsibility for Adam – they have two of their own, so that's understandable, especially when he's been paying maintenance for Christa as well. But the wife puts everything she can think of in the way of Harry ever seeing the boy. I'll try to talk to him at work tomorrow, tell him where Adam is, and maybe he can get down on the pretext of coming to see me."

"Where does he live?"

"Stevenage. Not much of a place, to my way of thinking."

"If you had a bet, what would you say is Peggy's game?"

"Satisfaction of a whim…Initially anyway. Very nice, very self-pleasing, perhaps just a bit of good fun. She was like that when I knew her – she and Harry came here often – and I've no doubt she's like that now. Never could look ahead, not even by a couple of hours. She's always enjoyed flirting with danger. That may be what she's doing now."

"That's exactly what I'm afraid of," said Graham.

And his unease increased as, day by day, they heard nothing whatever of Peggy.

10

Missing Persons

When Christa went back to Romford on the Monday Graham decided to spend the next few days getting to know Adam. This proved to be more difficult than he had expected. He got to know him rather as a bus-driver might say he had got to know a commuter. Adam was perpetually in and out, forever in transit, and since he fixed himself a sandwich whenever he needed food, they did little more than hail each other in passing. When Graham saw Adam in the outside world he seemed to be surrounded by two or three of an army of friends, always talking and laughing.

Graham remembered Christa saying on the night of the dinner that Adam didn't have friends as other people had them. If she was right then, there had been a miraculous transformation. Graham could not attribute it to himself, so he had to conclude that it was Adam's being liberated from Peggy that had had such a promising effect. He tried to put himself in Adam's mind to understand the change, but failed dismally. He wondered whether the change was only cosmetic – whether these boys he saw him with were not in fact "friends" even in the schoolboy sense, but only acquaintances, perhaps even fans. With the revival of sport as a national obsession prowess at any game probably scored highly in secondary schools. On the other hand, appearances were against such a reading of the situation. There was mutual pleasure in each other's company written over all their faces and bodies, and Adam was in or out of most of their houses every evening.

"You can bring your mates here whenever you want," he

said to the boy one evening.

"Oh, they'd like that, just to see what the writer's house is like," Adam said. "Just the once."

"Why only once?"

"Well, they've all got mums when we get hungry. I wouldn't want you to have to make food for that lot."

Graham didn't greatly fancy it either. And he was quite sure the food, by their lights, wouldn't be much good.

"I'm beginning to get worried about your mother," he said, the next evening, when Adam was just in and not quite off to bed.

"Are you? I never think about her."

Graham didn't think this was, or could be, true.

"It's over a week now. There may come a point when the police will find it odd if we don't make a bit of a fuss."

Adam considered this.

"She might have met up with that stupid long-lost son. Probably she's made it up with him, and they're all lovey-dovey somewhere or other in London."

"It's one of the possibilities. But when he left Luigi's he was almost as angry with her as you were."

After a few minutes Adam said:

"I'm sorry, I shouldn't have said that. Terry is your son."

"Apparently."

"And it's not surprising she's so happy, when he was her first child, and she was forced to give him up."

Graham remembered Ted Somers's mutter that there was no pressure on her from her parents.

"If she was forced to give him up," he said.

"Yeah, that's the thing…You have to look at everything she says, check it if you can, to see if it's true," said Adam at once. "I'm fed up with it."

That was as near as Adam came to opening his heart.

It was a great joy and relief to Graham that he did not have to consider Adam in any way as a suspect. If Peggy's body had been found in the streets of Romford the son whom she had so publicly quarrelled with would have to have been near the top of any policeman's list. But the idea of him meeting up with her, murdering her, then spiriting her away (how?) or finding a hiding-place for the body which kept her hidden for over a week – all these were not possibilities: they were beyond belief. Anyway he was probably with his friend Micky Leatherby and his parents at the relevant time, and then with Graham and Christa for the rest of the night.

"Is it all right if I go to Romford tomorrow?" Graham asked Adam the next day.

"'Course it is. I've got a key."

"There's one or two people I think I should talk to there. And then I'm wondering if I should go to the police."

"The police? I've thought about them since you mentioned them." He was all tensed up now. "Won't they wonder about us?"

"Well, I thought I could tell them that I'm a sort of step-father to you both. That should square things with them, and reassure them that you're safe and well. Like I said, I'm afraid of them getting suspicious if we report her disappearance, then don't give any sign afterwards that we're worried about her…I think I could handle them better than your grandfather."

"That wouldn't be hard!" said Adam. "He's not good with people. He gets on better with cars."

"How much has he had to do with your mother in recent years?"

Adam looked surprised.

"Nothing. I never remember him having anything to do with her. I'd never seen them together before that meal on Monday."

Adam had his hand on the door-handle, but Graham suddenly said:

"You do realize, Adam, don't you, that this is your home for as long as you want or need it to be? You and Christa, of course."

Adam shuffled.

"What? Oh, I thought maybe, but…I didn't *know*. I'm very grateful…Thank you."

And he scooted out of the door.

Graham immediately turned his novelist's analytical brain on himself. He couldn't decide why he had said this *now*. It seemed to have just come out. But it must have been lurking there somewhere in the back of his mind. He had promised Adam a home until adulthood. It couldn't have been just his burgeoning love for Christa that led him to make such a large commitment of himself, his time, his money. He decided he must, in an odd way, feel he had escaped his rightful burden of responsibility with Terry. He had not been told, of course, but would he have taken it up in any meaningful way if he had been told?

And now he was taking it up with Peggy's other two children. They had hauled themselves through childhood with no security and precious little love. Now at least he could provide the first, and in Christa's case the second too. For as long as she would let him. Until some other man took over that duty. He had never yet seen any indication from Christa that she had for a moment considered him in a romantic role.

Graham left a message at the home of Christa's friend Josie: he would pick her up at the Jeremy Bentham College at around five o'clock. The next day he drove to Romford, and as long as the country roads lasted he pondered what he was doing.

Peggy had 'disappeared' some time during the late evening or night of the previous Monday. He put the word disappeared in inverted commas in his mind because she had either been put out of commission in some way (kidnapped, killed, illegally detained), or she had gone off willingly. Considering the note she had left he rather inclined to the last explanation, but he had to admit that the situation could have developed dangerously later on.

This meant, surely, that the solution to the mystery had to lie in Romford. Peggy had left Luigi's intent on searching for Terry and making it up with him. Her intention presumably was to comb the streets of Romford until she found him. It was while doing this that she either herself decided to disappear (problems, emotional or financial, that only she knew about?), or was persuaded to go away, or forcibly taken. The last solution seemed to him unlikely: the message left in the house in Milton Terrace did not sound like a forced or dictated message. In fact it had sounded typically Peggy, as he, with his creative imagination, had come to see her. And it had been accepted by Christa as having been written by Peggy.

He realized that he was trying to view the situation as a policeman or a private detective might view it: dispassionately and logically noting all the pertinent features of the case and reviewing all the probabilities. He hoped he might be able to find a policeman in Romford who would view the facts from the same perspective but with more professional expertise and experience.

His first port of call, using his *A to Z*, was Ted Somers. He lived – alone now – in a bungalow on Silverdale Street, bought no doubt at the time when Peggy had wheedled the house in Milton Terrace away from him. The bungalow was neat and square, just the sort of manageable place a retired couple liked, and the garden was predictably well-cared-for. Ted had more time on his hands than he knew what to do with. That was also suggested when he opened the door.

"Mr Broadbent! I didn't expect —"

"Graham, please. I hope I'm not unwelcome."

"Not in the least. Come in. Coffee?"

"Please."

"There's some brewed. I live on coffee all morning to keep myself awake. What brings you here?"

"I'm fetching Christa from college this evening. But it's actually Peggy who brings me here."

"I could have guessed. It's getting worrying."

"You felt that too?"

"I did. Though I don't see it's your worry."

"It's the children's, or should be. Has she gone off with anyone for this long before?"

"Search me. I'd had nothing to do with her for over ten years, and until recently very little to do with the children. What do they say about her going off unexpectedly?"

"I've tried not to pry too closely. I do get the impression that it's longer than has happened before, but they're not too bothered."

"Used to it. Of course I gathered she sometimes went off, but I didn't press them too closely, probably for the same reasons you don't want to. I said we – Mary, when she was alive, and I – were there if they needed us, and left it at that. It looks like driving a wedge between mother and children if you make too much of things that shock you, and we always tried not to do that."

"I suppose there was a time, wasn't there, when you, your wife and Peggy were all living together? After Terry's birth and before Adam's?"

"All her life up to her marriage with Harry." He sighed as he handed over a large cup of coffee and sat down over his own. "I don't want to give you the impression it was just one man after another in her life. It wasn't. But the men in her life were mostly there for a short time. A few days, a few weeks. Between these periods she went on with her life perfectly normally: jobs, learning her parts for the Romford Players, *dreaming*…She always lived partly in a dream world. Somehow her life was going to be transformed: money, fame, a dream lover. We never really talked about it, never sat her down and told her to get a grip. We were a little bit in awe of her, I think, because she was so different from us, and from anyone in our families. And we knew it would have been hopeless. But she just let fall things that told us what was going on in that imaginative little head: some of the men were 'fabulously rich' – just ordinary local businessmen; some were 'fantastically handsome' – pleasant-looking; talent scouts were coming to the plays specially to see her. We recognised it as childishness, and we were embarrassed by it. The wonder is she kept anybody long enough to marry him and stay married for some years."

"So in those years she didn't have any relationship that was in some way special – lasted a while, seemed more serious?"

"Not that we knew of." He drank from his coffee. "Mind you, we didn't know much."

"Not even Christa's father?"

"We had no idea who he was…" As he thought, his elderly face unexpectedly crimsoned up. "We thought she didn't know herself."

"Why do you think that?"

"Because she never named anyone, or went after him for maintenance."

Graham digested this.

"She never came after me for maintenance."

"Probably because she figured there was no chance of getting any. In any case, the baby was adopted almost immediately."

"Maybe Christa's father was also an unlikely source of money."

"Maybe. The truth is, we were past caring. Christa's never showed any curiosity, and we thought – Mary and I – that that was much the best way. She somehow got the idea that you were her father, and we didn't tell her anything to the contrary, though Mary always said it was just a bit of Peggy's silliness. So far as we knew you and Peggy had never met up again."

"We didn't. I was in Mali at the relevant time."

"Africa somewhere? Peggy's never been to darkest Africa, I'm sure. It's not glamorous enough for her."

Graham drained his cup.

"So what were relations between you like in those years?"

Ted always thought before replying. He liked to make himself clear.

"More and more distant. We hardly seemed to have any share in her life or her dream world. When she teamed up with Harry and went to live with him in a flat near the station, we were surprised and delighted. We put on a lovely wedding for them, and were over the moon when Adam came along. It seemed like a replacement for the boy she'd had adopted. He was about two when she first brought up the idea of buying the house from us. You know the rest."

"She swindled both you and her brother, didn't she?"

"She did. She knew it was best to keep it in the family."

It was a sad little story. They talked for a bit longer. Ted was still full of the hole left in his life by his wife's death. After his beloved daughter failed him, Mary was his mainstay. Graham promised to keep in touch, and told him he was going to the police later, in an attempt to inject a bit of urgency into their concern.

The next stop was the Halliburtons – obviously Peggy's best friends in Romford. There were two or three customers in the shop, and Graham felt rather guilty at asking to speak to one or both of the pair.

"You go, Mike," said Vesta. "You know her best. Take him in the back room, then I can come in and have my say if we get slack in the shop."

So Michael Halliburton took Graham through to a little box of a room, with two easy chairs, a kettle and a hotplate-cum-grill. Graham refused more coffee and got down to business.

"I expect you think I'm causing a stir about nothing."

Michael shifted slightly uneasily in his chair.

"Well, I don't want to sound as if I don't care about Peggy. And she has been away longer than I expected, I'll admit that. It won't be long before rehearsals start for *Virginia Woolf.* But she is after all an adult, and we're not living in the nineteenth century."

"She has responsibilities," said Graham.

"Christa and Adam?" Michael gave a little laugh, and a dismissive wave of the hand. "But you'll have noticed that they're very self-sufficient, very grown up."

"What I noticed about Adam when I saw him first at Luigi's was that he is a typical adolescent, full of mixed-up emotions and a lot of resentment."

Michael shifted again.

"Well, I suppose so. Yes. But he'll have to learn to cope with that."

"He will. On his own, so far as I can see."

"I suppose you're saying Peggy is not much of a mother. Well, you're probably right, though she must be wonderful fun as well. What I've been more interested in is her acting ability, so maybe I have turned a blind eye to what you call her responsibilities."

"I suppose you would. No shame in that. But she's also a friend, isn't she?"

"Oh yes. Absolutely. That's why we got her working for us here. So we could keep an eye on her."

Not much of an eye, Graham thought.

"Mike, could you come out?" called Vesta from the shop. "We're busy."

Mike pulled himself up from his chair and hurried out. Graham thought he learned more about him from his movements than from his face, which was cleverly controlled. He was a man of energy – not the constant energy of a sportsman or athlete: the purpose and drive was in his shoulders and arms. When you saw the whole man in motion – as Graham now did, watching him serving two customers with notable efficiency and minimum movement – you saw someone who was egocentrically directed towards getting what he wanted, and getting it with minimum expenditure and unnecessary emotion. He must have been a first-rate director, Graham thought.

"Sorry about that," Michael said, coming back. Graham decided to chance his arm.

"You got Peggy working here to make sure no other amateur drama group poached her, didn't you?"

Mike smiled disarmingly (though Graham was not disarmed).

"Absolutely. No harm in that, is there?"

"None at all. Though it's not quite friendship, as it is normally understood."

"Two birds with one stone," said Mike airily. "There's drama groups all over South London would give their eye teeth to have her as a regular. Much of the reputation we've built up here has been due to her. Having her work in the shop, in a job which doesn't take much out of her emotionally – that's vital – and having her under our eyes makes her feel safe and us feel safe about her too."

Vesta, from the empty shop, poked her head around the door.

"And you've slept with her too, Mike. Might as well tell him, or someone else will. Didn't mean anything, and I wasn't jealous, but it happened."

The door-bell in the shop signalled a customer, and she disappeared. Graham raised his eyebrows at Mike.

"Yes, it happened. Well, it's happened now and again with one or two of our actresses. Like Vesta says, it doesn't mean anything. Our marriage is based on trust – the trust we both have that I'm *essentially* hers, and she's essentially mine."

Graham held back a sardonic comment. His own record as a married man disqualified him from making it.

"I see," he said. "I never quite managed to create that trust with my own wife." He chanced his arm on a guess again. "Did the parts she was playing make any difference to Peggy, in her actual life?"

Mike looked at him, thought, then laughed.

"Well, let's just say that playing Lady Windermere didn't make her into a virtuous, straight-laced wife. It doesn't work like that."

"I don't remember that playing St Joan turned her into a saint either."

"On the other hand, you could say that while she was rehearsing and playing Lady Windermere she became more formal in her manner, more queenly, more...remote. The onstage bearing got into the offstage behaviour to that extent."

"Yes...How long has it been decided that her next part will be Martha in *Who's Afraid of Virginia Woolf?*"

"Decided? Only two or three weeks before she took off. It's been in the air for a lot longer than that – as one of *her* parts, that eventually she'll have to play. She's about the right age now: still stunning when she makes the effort."

"I bet you've never said that to her."

"I certainly haven't. Why are you interested?"

"Martha. The woman who is so desperate to have a child that she and her husband create an imaginary son. And while Peggy is getting into the mood to start rehearsals of the play, into her life comes a real son..."

"That can only be coincidence."

"Oh, almost certainly. Though with the current enthusiasm for adoptive children contacting their birth mothers it was quite likely to happen, and while the child was still young...What struck me was that, while she's preparing to play a woman overflowing with maternal love and frustration in having no object for it, along comes a long-lost son. And she is over the moon, all over the boy, eager to share the news with all the world."

"Partly in preparation for the role, do you think?"

"She's never been particularly maternal with the two children she already has, according to them. And then, perhaps quite soon, the new son sees through the role-playing..."

Michael looked sceptical.

"Did you think he was particularly bright?"

"I didn't see enough of him to judge."

"And the reason for the bust-up was quite different."

"Yes, certainly. But also quite mystifying. Two potential birth fathers. It really calls for a judgment of Solomon, doesn't it?"

Graham got up.

"Where are you going now?" Mike asked.

"To the police."

"Is that necessary? Nothing we've said has given any reason why Peggy should have come to any harm."

"Maybe not. But a woman with a home, children, a job, a very exciting theatrical role in prospect, should be able to think of someone she should contact if she goes away unexpectedly. You and Vesta would be obvious people. But she hasn't. I'm just trying to get the police to put some urgency into the case. To do *something*."

That proved to be more difficult than Graham had imagined. The duty sergeant on the desk merely feigned interest: he pointed out it was not a child or an adolescent who had gone missing, and that grown adults were not required to register once a week at the police station. Even Mr Blunkett hadn't come up with that one. Graham felt inhibited from mentioning Peggy's children, so he pulled Peggy's other claim for special attention.

"She's a pretty well-known local figure. About the best-known amateur actress in Romford, regularly stars in the Romford Amateur Players shows. It will be a newspaper matter if she doesn't turn up soon."

The sergeant looked down at the computer record.

"Margaret Webster, known as Peggy. That rings a bell.

Would that be the lady who starred in *Hello, Dolly?*"

"Very likely."

"Brilliant she was. Not the greatest voice in the world, but oodles of personality."

"That sounds like Peggy. Do you go to the Romford Players' shows regularly?"

"Not regularly, no. But word usually gets around when there's something really good on. And this was top-notch. Good as the West End any day."

And this was enough to get the sergeant into the back room behind him and on the phone in low-voiced consultation with someone in the detectives' central office. Five minutes later Graham was in an informal interview room talking to a lean, sharp-eyed man, Detective Sergeant Relf, who was taking down details over and above what Ted had given them a few days earlier.

"Forty-three. Not the usual age for taking off with a bloke, but anything can happen – we learn that in this job. Somers was her maiden name, Webster the married one, is that right?"

"That's right."

"Husband no longer around?"

"No – lives in Stevenage with a new wife who dislikes him having contact with his earlier family."

"That's not unusual. And the children are in their teens, I see. That's a frequent reason for middle-aged parents just downing tools and going away for a bit. For a bit of a break, you might say. Who's looking after them?"

"I am. They're fine. I'm a sort of stepfather to them."

He was subjected to a sharp glance.

"So there'd been a relationship between you and her, then? When? Before or after the marriage?"

"Before. We were still in our teens. But there was a result: an elder brother for these two."

"I see. Now left home?"

"Yes, but not this home. He was put up for adoption at birth. He recently made contact with his birth mother. Peggy was delighted. Another reason for her not taking off suddenly."

Sergeant Relf raised his eyebrows sceptically.

"Maybe. But as far as I can see she did take off willingly. Mr Somers told us she left a note at her home to the children, saying she was going."

"That's right. 'With a friend' the note said."

"Sex unspecified, probably male."

"We've all assumed he's male."

"And what else did you assume? That she'd suddenly and unexpectedly met up with an old lover and gone off with him?"

"That seemed the most likely. But it's also possible she met a new man, there was an instant attraction, and they went off together. Unlikely but possible."

"As I say, we learn in this job that anything's possible. Now this meeting will have taken place just after there'd been some kind of celebratory meal at Luigi's in Cornwallis Street – is that right?"

"Yes. Between Peggy leaving Luigi's and her daughter and me finding the note at her house in Milton Terrace."

"Odd thing for a woman to do: go out and walk around in her home town after a meal."

"There'd been a bit of a contretemps."

"That would be a sort of disagreement or misunderstanding, would it, sir?"

The question was a reproof rather than an enquiry. Graham had not intended telling him about this, but now found himself doing so.

"Sorry. It was a minor row. Or perhaps 'scene' is a better word, because there was really only one person involved. The dinner had been to introduce her new-found son to her friends. His name is Terry Telford, by the way."

"Yes. I have it here. And there was Mrs Webster's father, a couple connected with the theatre group, her other two children, and you, sir."

"That's right."

"So you've remained friends over the years, have you, sir?"

"No. We'd only met up again recently, but I think she had remembered me and talked about me. I'm a novelist, and there is generally some publicity when a new book comes out. Anyway, she toasted Terry at the end of the meal, told us about giving him up when he was a baby, and so on. Then over coffee she got up again – Peggy likes being the centre of attention – and told the table that Terry had not only found his real mother, but also his father as well…She told them that I was his father."

"I see. Was this a surprise?"

"Not really. I'd suspected something like this was going to happen. I was beginning to understand Peggy."

"So what was the problem? Who made the scene?"

"Terry Telford. He said he already knew who his natural father was, and it wasn't me."

There was a silence. Sergeant Relf looked at him, eyes narrowed.

"Confusing for you, sir."

"Very."

"Upsetting? Would you have liked to be the father?"

"I'm a bit muddled on that matter. Think it over, Sergeant. You have a brief adolescent fling before your life has really started. Then twenty-five years later you find that the fling produced a son. Can you really care about him as you might do if you had known about him all along? I'm not sure that I can."

"Was Mrs Webster lying, or genuinely confused, do you think?"

"Sergeant, I only know one thing about Peggy: that you can never be sure about anything where she is concerned, and especially anything she tells you."

"As I said, confusing for you, sir. Well, sir, I'm definitely interested, but I'm not sure if I'm interested as a policeman or as a man. If you'll leave us your details I'll keep you informed if anything turns up. I'll treat you as temporary guardian of the children, who would in any case have to be informed."

"You say if anything turns up. That implies inactivity on your part."

"Not inactivity, though I can't see that the facts warrant very much zeal on our part. I'll do what I can. Shift the words around a bit: I'll keep you in touch if I turn up anything."

And with that Graham had to be content.

11

Dream World

Graham Broadbent was in a dream.

Not a sleeping dream, but a living, walking, seeing dream. He had taken Christa and Adam to see Kath Moores, whom they both liked. He left them in Bidford and then drove on to Upper Melrose. To the old Saxon Church beloved of architectural historians where he had first met, properly met, Peggy Somers, and to the churchyard where they had first made love, and perhaps made Terry Telford. Back to the beginnings of that brief, unremarkable affair that seemed, like so many things unremarkable in themselves, to have had such strange and long-lasting consequences.

He had already been round the church, all those years ago, noting all the features that the books had told him of, and all the changes that the more sophisticated medieval builders had made centuries after it was built. Sometimes he made jottings in a little architectural notebook which he kept with him on his excursions. They had had special hours at school with the headmaster – hours which had ranged over many subjects but often came back to English architecture, one of the head's pet subjects, and the one closest to his heart.

Eventually, in that summer of 1979, he had gone out into the sunlight, and that was when he saw Peggy. They had swapped words often, particularly in the wings during that first scene of *St Joan*, and he had thought how different, how wonderful, how unattainable she was. Now here he was in the churchyard, and here she was, sitting in the early evening light on a tombstone towards the further edge of the churchyard: Peggy Somers, the star of the school play, alone with him.

Twenty-five years later, walking round the churchyard and looking for *that* tombstone, Graham wondered about that meeting. It had too much of the coincidence about it – the sort of thing that most readers hated in novels. It would have been easier to accept, in a work of fiction, if Peggy had rung his home and been told by his mother where he had gone. But their acquaintanceship was not like that. She had been friendly in their backstage encounters, but she had not shown the slightest interest in him – not *that* way. And there were plenty in whom she had shown that sort of interest. She would never have rung his home. Two weeks after the performances of the play she would probably have been hard put to it to remember his name.

Finding the grave was not particularly difficult. The mental picture he had retained all those years was not too far from the reality, and in any case there were not many graves that had the shape and appearance of a tomb. It was the grave of Jonas Braithwaite, born June 14th 1827, died November 3rd 1893. And around the square structure the names of his wife Mary Ann, and their children, those who had died young and those who had grown up to live in what Graham imagined would have been the formidable shadow of their father.

Beside this grave, in the gathering twilight, they had made love.

Before that they had made the obligatory tour of the church itself. Graham pointing out interesting features to Peggy, she bored, hardly able to throw her eyes briefly in the right direction. When Graham had said that the church was centuries older than St Joan herself, Peggy had as near as dammit shrugged. St Joan was in the past.

They had gone out again, back to the tombstone. Both knew that at dusk someone would have to come and lock up the church. When they saw a man with an officious walk approaching from the village they had both, with unspoken unanimity, ducked down behind the tomb. They heard the door of the church open, imagined the inspection of the interior, then the door being locked.

"Hurry up, you silly old bugger," said Peggy, which shocked Graham, but gave him certainty about what was to occur next.

They peeped round the corner of the tomb and saw him emerge into the sunlight. They listened to his footsteps down the gravel path that bisected the churchyard, then they heard the clink of the lych gate. Then Graham's arm was around Peggy, she was looking up at the darkening sky, and they made love, and it was so much better, happier, more revelatory than it had been before for him that Graham almost fainted with happiness.

He realized at once that she was much more experienced than him.

Sitting now on the tombstone Graham wondered anew at the coincidence of their finding each other in such a place purely by chance. Had she come to Upper Melrose to meet up with a girlfriend (or boyfriend, come to that) and found the friend had gone on holiday, or away for the day? Had she got a holiday job in the village, and stayed on after the working day was over? That seemed unlikely. Even today, with attractive small villages mostly tea-shopped out of existence, Upper Melrose gave the appearance of having few jobs to offer even to residents. Saxon churches don't pull in the multitudes.

He wondered whether he had asked her at the time how she had come to be there. If so he couldn't remember her answer. He rather thought he had merely accepted her presence as a glorious gift from heaven to mark the end of his adolescence. He wondered if he would ever have the chance now to ask her.

If he did he could imagine her response: a shrug, and "Good heavens, how could I remember *that*?" Or perhaps a lie about a fabulously rich and handsome Lord of the Manor whom she had been visiting.

Around eight they went into the village. Peggy phoned her mother and said she'd been with her friend Katy and had missed the bus, and now she'd have to get the last one.

"You know me. Never have any idea of time," she said, and Graham got the idea this was an excuse used frequently with easily-bamboozled parents. Graham phoned his parents and just said he'd missed the bus. His parents didn't need to be lied to. He was a steady, responsible lad and they trusted him.

Then they went to the one dreary pub, the Grey Heifer, where they had a half of bitter and a shandy (Graham revelling in the new freedom of pub visiting, Peggy looking round at the smoky, brown-painted bar with contempt), and then they went back to the graveyard and the tomb of Jonas Braithwaite and made love again.

If only he could remember what they had talked about. Because they talked, in the intervals between the glorious sex. Probably they had talked about their parents, their futures, even their politics, if Peggy had had any (Graham had canvassed for the Liberals in the last General Election). Whatever it was it had been borne away on the breezes of memory. Only their comings-together remained.

And that had been it, really – or almost. There was the bus-ride home, and Graham did remember what they had talked about during its circuitous route to Bidford and Colchester. It had been the locals in the pub they'd just been in. Grim elderly men on their own, swapping monosyllables, two young men with slightly pathetic swaggers, and two airmen from the nearby American base, drinking silently, probably used to dreary bars. Peggy had observed all of them, and now took them off, endowing them with exaggerated Essex dialect, or an impossible American drawl, and putting preposterously gnomic utterances into their mouths. Graham thought she was wonderful.

"Is yer mum's raspberries roypened yit?" she would ask. Or: "The badgers be hot as billygoats this summer. 'Twill be a sad harvest." Graham couldn't wait to see her again.

They did meet again, three more times. Twice in the Colchester Castle Park, once on the deserted Grammar School sportsfield, where Graham was more active than ever he had been on sports' afternoons. Peggy never asked him home, or even floated the possibility. In fact she answered his phonecalls with the off-hand efficiency of a doctor's receptionist, all but saying "I think I could fit you in on Thursday afternoon." It didn't act as a passion-killer, but once the affair was over it left a slight feeling of resentment.

It finished with Peggy saying she was busy for the next fortnight and she'd give him a call. She never did, and he never rang her. Over was over, and there never was an affair more over than theirs. He was very conscious that it had fizzled out rather than exploded, and he felt ashamed of the fact.

During what remained of the summer Graham rethought his decision not to go to university. He did that mainly because he couldn't think of what else to do. He secured a late place at London University, and that was his next three years decided. He was a good but not outstanding student, and his main impact was as editor of the student newspaper, which he transformed into something that the students wanted to read and actually enjoyed. By the time he went out into the great world he knew that what he wanted was varied experience, and why he wanted it was to transform it into fiction. He went

into a management training programme, had a year with
Sainsbury's, another year with Christian Aid in Mali, and all
sorts of little bits and pieces after that. By 1987, when his first
novel was published, he had a fine stack of memories – places,
people, situations, to be moulded to his purposes.

He sometimes wondered whether his affair with Peggy had
been more fateful than it had seemed at first. Had it set a
pattern for his emotional life thereafter: short, sharp affairs
with minimal emotional involvement? Only he did not see
the one with Peggy as having been cold and distant. He had
carried the image of Peggy with him for years, and the
memory of her passion and her laughter came back at
disconcerting moments. That was why as soon as Christa had
mentioned the name in his hotel room in Colchester he had
been brought up short.

He sighed and wandered slowly out of the churchyard. The
village pub was now called The Pink Cockatoo, and
proclaimed a varied bar menu. He ordered a pint of bitter and
looked down the sandwich list, but when he tried to order he
was told that they didn't serve sandwiches on a Sunday. What
the various locals in pastel-coloured casuals were eating was
'Seared sea-bass with Duchesse potatoes and chanterelles' or
'Pigeon breasts in anisette sauce with mange-tout and parsnip
mash.' He'd almost have preferred the brown paint and the
threatening-looking locals. He downed his pint and left.

12

Body

It was one week before that the two boys had made their way from Hurst Green in Brightlingsea, down a narrow street on the far end of the small seaside town, then down a smelly lane and on to the mudflats where they played when they were bored or in disgrace at home. It was Sunday afternoon, and a watery sun was in the sky. Tim was the leader – not hyperactive, but active enough, his parents thought. Wayne was the follower and thinker.

Once they were down on the mudflats they were in their element, jumping from one cake of mud, with its rough marine vegetation, to the next one, then further and further out towards the river. On their way they pushed each other over, paddled in the little streams, and shouted vaguely rude remarks at the people with their dogs who were doing a Sunday walk from the Hard. It had been a dry couple of weeks, and the river had diminished to hardly more than a trickle. Some old boats were caught in a permanent dry or mud dock. Further away there were the wrecks of small craft and rowing boats that had been abandoned by their owners long ago.

These boats were the cherished goals of Tim and Wayne when the river was low enough for them to attain them without getting too wet. Once over the side they would play around in them, fantasizing as pirates, mutineers or boy-adventurers on the high seas. Now the receding line of the river left only little rivulets and puddles among the flats and gave them effective leave to roam over the whole area, with protests only from the seagulls whose all-purpose indignation was too well-known to frighten the boys.

Clouds were flickering, the light becoming more ambiguous, when they gained a decaying motor-boat long since wrecked, with its structure becoming more and more exposed to weather and to whatever passing scrutiny there was. Tim jumped on to the prow and put out his arm to help Wayne up too. Wayne was smaller, and sharper.

"Tim!"

Tim caught the note in his voice. He saw nothing, but swung his head round in the direction of Wayne's finger.

"Fookinell," he said. It was his father's ultimate expression of shock or disgust. Then he said: "It's a woman."

"'Course it's a woman," whispered Wayne. "She's wearing a petticoat…Is she dead?"

"She's dead all right," said Tim, with pretended confidence. "Can you see her breathing? Come on – we've gotta get home. Keep quiet about this or we'll be in trouble."

But it wasn't as simple as that. They sped back home, and Wayne was put in a bath and given dry towels while Tim's parents let him dry out and then hacked the mud off him.

"Tim's very quiet," said his mother to his father.

"Makes a nice change," said his dad.

But he was very quiet on Monday too, and at night his father heard him cry out in his sleep. On Tuesday his parents were going up to bed and heard him sobbing in his room, but the next day he said there was nothing wrong. It was only on Thursday that he said to his mother:

"We saw a body."

She stopped what she was doing.

"What do you mean, a body?"

"It was a woman. In a boat down by the river. We thought she was dead."

"Oh darling, you've got it wrong. She must have been sleeping. You know all sorts get on the flats. Probably been drinking. Just put it out of your mind."

"I don't like thinking of her lying out there."

Soon both parents realized that he hadn't and couldn't put it out of his mind. By the next Sunday his mother said to his father: "You'd better go and take a look. Do it today. It'll be nothing, and it'll put his mind at rest."

"But Manchester United's playing Chelsea this afternoon."

"*Go*. Go now. I'll hold up the dinner."

So, led by Tim, his father took the path down by the sewage stream, then out on to the mud – still very dry and overgrown – and out to the skeletal wooden wreckage of the small boat. This time it was Tim who pointed.

"F–," began his father, then thought better of it.

He swallowed, then decided what to do. He turned, put his arms around the boy's shoulders and hastened back across the mud. There was to be no Sunday dinner that day till the roast pork was well dried out and all appetites were gone. As a rule the police presence in Brightlingsea was, in the locals' opinion, as useless as an answerphone but after a frustrating series of transfers to one after another low-level policemen, a promise was made that a car would be sent. They picked up Tim's father, and he took them down to the river and pointed over the flats to the boat.

He was talking to them for the rest of the day, and from his window as he went to bed he could see lights on the flats, a canvas arrangement, and the shadowy shapes of the SOCO men and women going about their grisly business.

Graham was beginning to wonder whether the children's grandmother had been as good as her word about telling her son Harry where Adam and Christa were, when he rang him.

"You don't know me. I'm Harry Webster. I was married to —"

"Peggy, of course. You're Adam's father."

"Yes. My mother tells me you're looking after the children, and doing it very well. I'm enormously grateful."

"I'm not sure I'm doing it well. I have no experience, and I'm sure to be making mistakes. But I'm doing what I can. Christa is not a child any more, by the way."

"No, of course not. I just meant Peggy's children…I gather that she's taken off."

"Yes. That's what we've assumed. I'm beginning to think it could be more serious than that."

"I see…Things are very difficult at this end."

The words came out hangdog and embarrassed. Graham didn't take to the man.

"So I gather," he said. "Would there be any less objection from your wife to your seeing Adam if she knew that Peggy's not in the picture at the moment?"

"Maybe…Just a little. But that's not the major objection. Shirley's not unreasonable, but we have our own family now. You can see she wouldn't want to be landed —"

"And you can see that Adam is unhappy at being regarded as a burden to be avoided or shunted off as quickly as possible."

"Oh, I didn't mean —"

"Particularly as his mother generally had interests more pressing than her children."

"Oh, she did. Peggy was a quite awful mother sometimes." Graham left a silence. Some inklings of Adam's difficulties during his growing-up period seemed to dawn on Harry.

"I'm fairly free tomorrow."

The voice sounded less than heroic, and even less than fully decided. But Graham seized on it.

"When could you come down? I'd like to have a talk with you myself."

"Early afternoon? I could have a bit of time with Adam then, when he finishes school. I can tell Shirley I'm kept late."

So Graham gave his usual direction – "three down from the general stores" – and rang off.

He was unsure what to expect from Harry Webster, but he certainly didn't anticipate a strong mind. Adam's force and obstinacy probably came from his Webster grandmother. When he told the boy to come straight home Adam's face first lit up but only for a second. Then the lowering expression that had recently disappeared from his repertory of looks took its place.

Harry rang the doorbell at ten-past two on Tuesday, shook hands genially and accepted Graham's offer of a cup of coffee. He had obviously had a pub lunch, along with the maximum allowed quantity of beer. He was slim, tallish and naturally good-humoured, but the lack of backbone showed in ineffectual gestures and an inclination to shy away from awkward questions as soon as they came up. Shirley obviously had an easy victim.

"I know of you, of course," he said, sitting down with his cup. He didn't seem to mean primarily Graham's reputation as a novelist.

"Peggy told you I was Christa's father, I suppose?"

"Well, yes."

"I'm not. Peggy's and my brief affair – if it's not dignifying it to call it an affair – was six years earlier."

"But why did she…? Oh, I suppose she put that around because you're quite well known. She had to use and broadcast the fact that you and she had…been together."

"That's right. Or rather that's what I guess. She was cagey on the subject when I talked to her recently. I think we both know Peggy well enough to take everything she says with a pinch of salt."

"I suppose we do. And the children do too. They're under no illusions."

"No. But I feel very sorry for them. It is confusing to have a mother who habitually fantasizes or tells downright lies."

"Yes, I imagine it is. But my mother says they're taking her absence very well."

"So far. But though they're sceptical about Peggy, I don't sense any downright hostility. So they're bound to be worried underneath."

"I'm sure they are. Any idea who she's gone off with?"

"I've been out of her life for twenty-five years. I wondered if you might have more ideas."

Harry thought about this, wondering whether to shy off and deny all knowledge. But by and by he decided it would be easier to face up to the question.

"I suppose she could have met up with anyone from her past life."

"Or her present. But you'll know most about her past."

"Yes." His mind was searching in that past for names. "She slept now and then with Michael Whatsit from the players, who was her favourite director. Oh, you know about that. There was a Romford businessman called…called Meyer, I think. There was the odd besotted fan, and a boy much younger than herself who played for Romford United…I'm not being much help, am I?"

"I can't say at this stage. I'd like to hear about someone who really stood out. Someone whose affair with her was something special, for her or for him, or both."

"Was there such a person? If so I never heard of him. It was all brief flings, one-night stands or at most one-month ones. Nothing you could call serious."

Graham was struck again by a resemblance to his own sex life.

"I did wonder about Michael Halliburton."

"That's the name!" said Harry. "He was just one of two or three people in the RAPs who were directors. He was her favourite. But she probably slept with the other two as well. The RAPs haven't caught up yet with women directors."

"I wondered about that. I thought it might be like Ingrid Bergman always sleeping with her leading man of the moment – only with directors instead. But then I wondered if Michael Halliburton could be Christa's father."

Harry Webster considered this.

"It would tie up with one thing."

"What's that?"

"She never received any maintenance for Christa."

Graham thought for a moment.

"Until she got it out of you."

"That's right. You could say I was a fool to adopt her —"

"I expect your wife says exactly that."

"Over and over, and even though I've ceased having to pay. I liked Christa, thought she had talent. But if it was Michael, slapping a maintenance order on him might have soured the relationship, and Peggy relied on him for good parts, and for the sort of coaching and bullying that made her successful in them."

"And Vesta could have taken the affair a lot more seriously than she pretends to."

But Harry was dubious about that.

"Maybe. But I've never seen any sign of that. She works with Peggy in the shop, and surely it would have come out. I think it's a genuinely open marriage. As ours was."

"On principle?"

"No, in practice. When Peggy started playing away, I felt I could do the same. It was messy, but it worked for a while."

"But you had to be mother and father to the children, I would guess."

"Something like that. I suppose Peggy cared about them both, in her way. But she never cared *for* them, never felt responsible for them."

"And you can't take responsibility for Adam now."

It was not a criticism, just a statement. An expression passed over Harry's face.

"No way. No chance at all." He swallowed. "I love my wife. Don't get me wrong. But it wouldn't be fair on Adam. She'd make his life hell."

"You have children, you and Shirley, don't you?"

"Oh yes. But they're still young. They'll be kept on a tight rein. That's Shirley's way. Adam never has been. It simply couldn't work."

They were interrupted by a key in the front door, and its opening. Adam rushed through into the front room.

"Dad!"

Harry had stood up. He raised his arms and Adam ran into them. Graham was surprised to note that Adam was as tall as his father. As he got up to go into the kitchen and leave them alone he got a glimpse of the shot so dear to producers of soap operas: the shot of an embrace, one face seen above the other figure's shoulder, and the face showing doubt, or hatred, or obsession – some emotion that we know the other figure isn't aware of and doesn't share. The expression on Adam's face was doubt and disillusion. He was experiencing the lack of warmth in the embrace.

Graham fiddled and fussed for as long as possible in the kitchen. When the coffee was ready he took it in on a tray, muttered something about biscuits, then left them to it again. There was conversation going on, but it seemed to be mostly question and answer, and it lacked passion. Back in the kitchen he found some chocolate and some ginger biscuits and put them on a plate. There was some panetone in the bread tin, and he sliced it and buttered it, as Adam liked it. He was just taking it in when the telephone rang in the study.

"Graham Broadbent speaking."

"Ah, Mr Broadbent. This is Sergeant Relf here."

Graham felt a sinking feeling in his stomach.

"Do you have some news?"

"Maybe, and maybe not. Does Brightlingsea mean anything to you?"

"I've been there. It's a little seaside and yachting place about ten miles from Colchester. I seem to remember two of the characters in a Graham Greene novel having a dirty weekend there. It doesn't seem likely, but I suppose he would know. It's the yachting that it's known for."

"I was really asking: did it have any associations with Peggy Webster?"

"With Peggy? Not that I know of, but it's within fairly easy reach of Bidford where she used to live."

"Only there's been a body found there. Woman of about the right age. The body's been in a little wrecked motorboat on the flats there for some time – two weeks or more, they think."

"I see. Have you told Ted Somers?"

"Yes. He's going down to Colchester, to the police morgue there. He's taking his son with him. I think he's pretty shaken by the news. I'd guess he always expected her to turn up."

"Well, apparently she has before. You sound as if you're fairly sure it's her."

"Not fairly sure. But we've e-mailed them the photo we had and they think it could be. I wondered if you would care to be there when the Somerses see the body."

"I don't know about that. Ted and the brother know her far better than I do. But I'd like to be there for Ted, if he's upset. I've got a lot of respect for him."

"They expect to be at Colchester Police Headquarters about seven tonight."

"I'll be there…I just hope it's not her."

"Well naturally. So do her family, I'm sure. But I wouldn't get your hopes up too high."

"It seems so unlike Peggy. To go out with a whimper like that."

As he put the phone down he heard the front door closing. He regretted he had not shut the study door. When he went into the front room he found Adam crying. He was willing to bet it wasn't for his mother.

13

Sitting in Judgment

When Graham arrived in Colchester it was nearly seven o'clock in the evening. Parking was easy to find, and when he made himself known at Police Headquarters he was told that the two Mr Somerses had arrived five minutes before. He was taken through to the waiting room outside the mortuary by a fresh-faced young constable who looked as if he was playing truant from school.

The two Mr Somerses mentioned were sitting on a bench – together but apart. Ted was bent forward, his face in his hands. His son was staring at the wall opposite, his face granite. When he saw Graham approaching he got up and went to meet him.

"I think you must be Graham Broadbent. I'm Oliver Somers. It was good of you to come."

"I just thought your father might need all the support he could get. It's going to be difficult for him."

"It's difficult for him now," said Oliver, gesturing. "For all of us. The emotions are so…mixed."

He was, Graham guessed, not much older than himself. It suddenly seemed strange that he knew so little about him. If people had mentioned him at all the references had been unspecific. He was sturdy, with plenty of flesh on him, but no feeling to him of comfort or relaxation. Restless, questing – someone, Graham felt, who didn't easily make do with second-best or with slipshod work or dubious standards. Graham's thoughts were interrupted by a police sergeant emerging from a door at the far end of the room and coming to fetch the two men to the mortuary. If he had actually dragged his feet Ted could hardly have been more obvious in showing his reluctance. Mixed emotions or not, grief and regret were now clearly in the ascendant. Walking beside him, Oliver offered his father his arm. It was rejected gently.

Graham sat down on the bench, and it was now his turn to stare at the opposite wall. Somehow he had no doubt that the body was Peggy. Perhaps it was Essex that seemed conclusive to him: here she was, in her ending, back in the area that had started her on her rackety life of lying, fantasy, making waves and disastrous relationships.

The door at the far end opened again. It was obvious he was right the moment he saw Ted and Oliver's figures in the doorway. Ted seemed to have shrunk, his shoulders to have become still more bowed where once they had been square and straight. He and Oliver talked to the police sergeant, then Ted went off with him and Oliver came over.

"Ted's going to give his account of that last night," he said, "the one in the restaurant. The sergeant's agreed that we can go, since we probably haven't got much to add. They think this case will be handled mainly by the Romford police, but they'll be going into how and why the body was found around here, whether she was known here, whether anyone remembers her being here around the time of the disappearance. I've told Dad we'll be in the nearest pub, which is the Crown. Is that OK?"

"Of course. I want to give any support I can."

"The children are OK?"

"Yes. Well, not entirely. Christa is always all right of course, being so in control of herself and everyone else. She's in Romford living with a friend most of the week. Adam's just had a visit from his father, and it didn't go well. But he's resilient, even if he's not as tough and together as he thinks. He'll be with friends. I told him I might not be back till tennish."

The Crown was a pub of the brass lamp and funeral parlour walls variety, and it was too early for it to be crowded. Graham got two pints and they found themselves a table where they could talk privately. Oliver reverted to the matter of Adam.

"How do you think he will react to his mother's death?" he asked.

Graham thought.

"I don't know…I've given up making assumptions about the lad. He may feel very uncertain at the moment, though he gives the impression that he lives for the day, and fits into whatever the circumstances of the time are. That's upbringing and training, I suppose. I gather Peggy's time was always her own, rather than her children's. He must be wondering what the next few years have in store for him, not to mention where I fit in."

Oliver looked at him hard.

"So what do the next few years hold for him?"

"Possibly going to live with your father – especially if he marries Kath Moore and comes back to live in Bidford. Or alternatively staying on with me. Possibly commuting between the two: he seems to have settled well into school at Hepton Magna, and he could go to his grandfather for weekends."

"You've no connection with him though, have you?"

Graham shook his head.

"None at all. I've never had children, and though I'm not conscious of having missed anything, I wouldn't say no to having responsibility for one I liked for a few years. How about you?"

Oliver jumped.

"I'm…well, pretty much in the same position as yourself. But my job – I'm in insurance – takes me away a lot. And I've virtually never met the boy. I was leaving my father's one evening when he and Christa arrived on a visit. Hail and farewell. Frankly, I don't relish the idea of taking him on."

"I didn't suggest that you should, only that you might welcome the opportunity. One thing Adam doesn't need at this stage is a reluctant guardian."

Oliver gazed gloomily into his still-full glass.

"You make me sound like a real bastard."

"Not intentionally."

"Perhaps there's no other way it could sound. But not knowing the lad, and never having had anything to do with Peggy for the last ten years or more…"

"That would be when she cheated you over the house sale?"

"Yes. She had just got married, it was soon after Adam's birth. I liked Harry Webster so far as it went, which wasn't very far. He got on all right with Christa, brought in a reasonable income, and Peggy and he seemed fairly happy. So there were good omens for the whole family, and I was willing to throw in a contribution to making things work. I had made a nice little nest-egg from buying shares during the privatisation boom and selling them before things went sour. The money would go direct to Dad, would provide him and Mum with a really stable last few years, and it would come back to Peggy and me when they died."

"Only it never got to him, did it?"

"No." He shifted in his seat. "That was the first inkling I had that Peggy was slippery about money, with no conscience about how she got hold of it. Before I'd just lent her the odd few pounds that never came back, but this was something else. As soon as I learnt what had happened – from Dad, who was absolutely bowled over, and really bitter and sad – I cut off ties entirely. Quite apart from anything else, I knew I had been made a fool of, and it would have done me no good for that to get around at work. I never felt the smallest urge to make any advances, try for a reconciliation with her. So there's been no contact between me and the children."

"But it's brought you closer to your father."

"To Dad *and* to Mum. You never met her, I gather. She was a wonderful woman. Dad had been in the garage trade, and he knew about dodgy dealings, even if he never went in for them himself. Mum was straight as they come, and warm and amusing too."

"But they both had made a favourite of Peggy as a girl?"

Oliver almost flinched.

"Yes...You can't blame them − she was so sparkling, had such life...I could understand her being Daddy's girl: that was a thing one saw so often, and felt was only natural. But Mum was just as besotted. I was only a year or so older, and though I loved Peggy too, and thought she had wonderful talents, I could see through her on the human level, and I knew she twisted them round her little finger. That was something they eventually found out when they only got half the money for the house...It was good to see a lot of Mum in her last years, and it's been good to see close up what a fine, decent man Dad is, what strength he has shown through it all."

"Here he is."

He didn't look strong now. He skirted the little knots of drinkers, his eyes going everywhere, his stoop still more pronounced. He nodded to Graham and sat down, saying nothing. He seemed to be oppressed by a great burden of misery and memories. To leave him and his son together Graham got up and fetched him a drink from the bar. He didn't have to ask him what he wanted. Ted was a beer man. Only when he had downed a quarter of the glass did some kind of life appear in his eyes.

"God, I needed that," he said. "I haven't needed one so much since Mary died."

"What did they want to know, Dad?" Oliver asked. Ted seemed to struggle to find a memory of the last half-hour.

"Oh, the party at Luigi's. Why she left, and what she was going to do. What we did afterwards...I'd been over it all before, when I reported her missing at Romford."

"I've been over it too," said Graham.

"Well, that's police work. They have to do it, apparently – go over and over the same things...But these people also wanted to talk about her ties with round here."

The two younger men thought about that.

"You mean with Essex? With the Colchester area?" asked Graham.

"Yes. I really had to puzzle my brain. Of course she was brought up not so far from here, and went to school there. I told them about that. But had she had any connection with the area since she moved with us to Romford?" He looked at his son, who shook his head.

"Not that I know of, but then I *wouldn't* know, not about recent years. There's been no communication. I don't know of any connection in the years after we moved, but I only lived at home now and then, as you know, Dad."

"I'm a contact," said Graham. "I'm a sort of relic of her years living in Bidford."

"But you only came back into her life a few weeks ago," said Ted.

"Long enough, if you're scraping around for suspects."

"Do you keep up contacts with Colchester as a rule?" asked Oliver.

"No. My parents are both dead. I have no links. I came back about seven or eight weeks ago to go to a school reunion. It was in the local paper, and it was that that brought Christa to pay me a visit. It was a birthday party for the man who directed Peggy in *St Joan*."

"George Long. I remember him," said Ted. "He's still alive, is he?"

"Yes, very much so. But he's eighty-two, so I don't think they'll be looking at him as a suspect."

"I wasn't meaning —"

"There was one of the old boys there – he was in *St Joan* as well, and so was I – who got both sentimental and aggressive at the thought of Peggy. But I never got the impression that he'd had anything to do with her since that time."

Neither Ted nor Oliver felt this was a very fruitful source of speculation.

"I was back here a few days ago," said Graham, the thought suddenly coming to him. "To see Adam's grandmother in Stanway."

Ted nodded.

"Peggy used to get on well with her," he said. "She and Harry used to visit her quite often."

"So she could have made local contacts then," said Graham. "Was Harry from round the Colchester area?"

Ted shook his head.

"I don't rightly remember, but I think his mother moved to Stanway from Romford, as a lot of people do move to this area when they retire or are widowed: it's a bit cheaper, and a lot quieter. Anyway, Peggy and Harry met in Romford, I do remember that. She was in a pub with the acting crowd after a rehearsal. Harry wasn't one of that mob, not then or after, though he did a few odd jobs for them now and then because he was always handy."

"So what happened? Did they just get talking?"

"Either he picked her up, or she picked him up," said Ted, back in his scales-fallen-from-eyes mode.

"Graham, did Harry come with you and Adam to see his mother?" asked Oliver.

"Not a chance. He's under orders from his wife to see as little of Adam as possible. She has him completely under her thumb, apparently. He was paying a secret, snatched visit to Adam earlier today, but when he heard me talking on the phone to the police about the body at Brightlingsea he took off like a rocket."

The father and son looked at each other, but said nothing.

"Isn't it sad?" said Oliver eventually. "Dad and Mum were ideal parents, nothing too much trouble, always there when they were needed. And all they produce is a boring insurance man and a fantasist whose only interest was in herself. And yet she and Harry – he may just be weak, but Peggy! – apparently produce or at least bring up strong kids, full of character and basically decent and honest, if Dad is to be believed. If you'd looked at her you'd have said there was no way she should have had those two."

"Three," said Graham. Ted and Oliver looked abashed.

"Of course, three," said Oliver. "But Peggy couldn't get either credit or blame for – what's his name?"

"Terry Telford," said Graham. "No, I suppose she couldn't. I just mentioned him to emphasize that he does exist, was around on the night, and yet we seem to have forgotten him. I don't suppose the police have."

"I mentioned him to the police today," said Ted. "And before, at Romford. I expect they'll get on to him now, but I can't say they showed any special interest. Maybe they think he hasn't been around Peggy long enough to work up any sort of…resentment, rage, whatever it is that can make a man murder."

Oliver shifted uneasily in his seat, as one who had known Peggy long enough to have a rich supply of those emotions.

"The meeting between him and Peggy was presumably only the culmination of something, of a search," said Graham. "And the search itself may have been fuelled by rage or resentment."

"Odd about the two fathers," said Ted.

He was voicing the feelings of all of them, but, strangely, it was something that Graham, in his concern for the wellbeing and futures of Christa and Adam, had spent little time musing on.

"I only heard about that from Dad on the phone," said Oliver. "Let me get it straight in my mind. According to Peggy you were the father of Terry Telford."

"Yes," agreed Graham. "When I had the only talk with her alone that I've had since schooldays she said 'It was a boy, you know. A baby boy.' I could have guessed it was a baby. And then Terry appeared out of the Internet into her life: he was the right age and it was clear – it seemed clear to me – that I was his father."

"Though there's the complication, isn't there, that Christa also thought you were her father?" asked Oliver.

"I don't think that's much of a complication. First of all I was away in Mali in 'eighty-three to 'eighty-four, when she must have been conceived. Between Terry's birth and Christa's I'd made a very tentative start as a novelist. By the late Eighties, when Peggy might begin to talk to Christa about her parentage, I was getting nominated for fiction prizes and mentioned in lists of promising young writers. Having given away for adoption a possible status-symbol and talking point, Peggy just transferred the paternity to the younger child. I think that's very much in line with her usual approach to the truth."

"She came up with much more fantastic stories than that in her time," agreed Ted. "But have you thought: if having you as the father of one of her children is a status symbol, she could have made up your fathering of Terry too. You and she had…been together, but that in itself isn't much of a story, and it only gets really interesting and believable if there was a child as the result."

The younger men both pondered this.

"What did she say at the time?" Graham asked. Ted leaned forward and put his face in his hands.

"She said it could have been a lot of people. Well, 'several' was how she put it. Her mother and I couldn't believe our ears. Our darling girl! It was the shame of thinking that some of her men could be local that decided us: we had to move. And Romford seemed the ideal place: big and sort of anonymous, a London suburb. A child of uncertain father wouldn't make the sort of stink there that it would in Bidford."

"But she didn't mention my name?" Graham asked.

"No. She mentioned boys in the school play, local men, but she never put a name to them. Said it wouldn't be right. Maybe she couldn't."

"So along comes Terry, and he's handed over for adoption to the Telfords. Were they told anything about the father?"

"Search me. She did all that herself. I think she went through the regular channels though. She had phonecalls at home from the Social Services people – whatever they were called then. Or said that's who they were from"

All three men sat thinking, all of them out of their depths. Even Ted, it seemed, had tried to have as little as possible to do with Peggy's first pregnancy and birth. Graham turned to Oliver.

"You never asked Peggy about the father of her son?"

"Not on your life! I was twenty, very inexperienced, and thoroughly ashamed of my sister. Also by then I knew I couldn't rely on getting a truthful answer out of her, so what was the point of asking?"

Silence descended again.

"Let's shift the focus away from Peggy," said Graham at last. "Young Mr Telford says he knows who his natural father is. How does he know? Maybe by going on the Internet. That's how he got in touch with Peggy. Why try to find your father *first*? Most people are more interested in their mother. The mother has had more to do with the child, inside and outside of the womb. Often there's a pathetic story involved. With the father it's more likely to be a rather grubby tale of cowardice or dereliction of duty. But Terry goes after the father first – or so far as we can tell he does. He'd only known his mother for three weeks or so before she vanished out of his life."

"There's another thing," said Oliver. "You've a much better chance of finding your mother. A father may not even know he *is* the father of such a child – as you didn't, Graham – or he may not want to be identified for financial or other reasons. Many people would say there isn't quite the same bond as between a mother and her child, so a strong wish to form a close relationship is rarer."

"All this leaves us with a mystery," said Graham. "Why, how, and when did Terry come to find his father – if that's what he is – before he found his mother?"

"Ask the lad himself," said Ted. "There's no reason for him to be embarrassed or ashamed. Why should he clam up?"

"Why indeed?" said Graham. "But that just could be connected to Peggy's death, so we ought to go carefully."

"We?" said Oliver. "Is there a we? If so, I don't think I'm part of it. We should just leave it to the police."

"Aren't you curious who murdered your sister?"

Oliver thought, then shook his head.

"Hardly at all, to be honest. When you haven't had any contact for years, and when you've been done down by her…Well, it's difficult to care."

"I think this is a *plot* to you," said Ted, to Graham's surprise. "Not a story of real people, but a story, like you might use in a book. I didn't get the impression you cared much about Terry Telford."

"I didn't."

"He's just one of the pieces in the jigsaw to you."

"Maybe. But I care about Christa and Adam."

"But what will happen to them?" Oliver asked. "How can you claim to be their guardian or foster-father? You've no connection with them?"

"You talk as if people are queuing up," said Graham. "I think that if I'm *in situ*, if Adam is happy, and if Christa is with us at least part of the time – there's no question of her legally needing a foster home, but she'd be a stabilising factor for Adam – I think the Social Services people will be ready to rubber-stamp the arrangement."

"I hope you're right," said Oliver feelingly.

"And I'm grateful, and will be quite willing to play a part," said Ted.

"Look, I care for both of them. And I also care about the truth coming out – in an abstract way, I think: that people are better for facing up to truth. So I may follow up trails that I think the police won't be interested in. By the way, Ted: there's no doubt that it is murder, is there?"

"No. Strangulation," said Ted, getting up. "No disrespect, Graham, but Peggy, even after what she's done, could never be a piece in a jigsaw to me. Not after I've seen her on the slab, seen the marks on her throat…I think I need to go home and have a rest, Oliver. I'm absolutely dead-beat."

Oliver jumped up, very ready to depart. They clearly wanted to be on their own. On their own together, or actually on their own, Graham wondered? He raised his hand in farewell, gave them five minutes, then left the Crown to find his way back to his car.

His brain was less tired than his body, and as he walked he reviewed the evening. Ted, he felt sure, had only had half his mind on the conversation. The rest of his mental faculties had been back in the nineteen-seventies, reviewing the death of a daughter he had once had, or thought he had, rather than that of the middle-aged woman who had given him so much grief. Oliver was more difficult to fathom. Like his namesake he seemed to want *more*: more love, which he had had too little of in childhood, more respect, more of life's rewards. Had he cast aside his sister too readily, Graham wondered, and had the motive been jealousy more than the feeling of having been swindled by her?

When he got home Adam was just back from an evening with his friends, seemingly restored to normality by the elasticity of youth. This time Graham did not just accept this gratefully and hope for the best. Telling him about his mother's death enabled him to make a point again with force and sincerity.

"As long as you need it or want it, you have a home here," he said.

Adam nodded, apparently sincerely grateful, and Graham was glad he had done something that was dictated by no self-interest or ordinary logic. He didn't ask himself whether his offer to Adam was really a covert offer to Christa.

As he went to bed, a stiff whisky later, his mind was on someone else: the young man who was apparently his real son. One thing he was going to have to find out was how Terry had acquired a father who was not him. And that, surely, meant he was going to have to revise his decision about talking to the Telfords.

14

Parenting

Graham had a great deal to think about in the days that followed. Adam was not a problem: he had accepted his mother's death coolly, as Christa had too, and he resumed his nonchalant approach to whatever befell him, though this did not deceive Graham, and he was conscious all the time of the need to provide a bedrock of stability for the boy. But he was also thinking of his other near-son, and the need to get into some contact with him. Much thought produced the conviction that he should not approach Terry before he had a better idea of what the Telfords were like, and what kind of upbringing he had had. And approaching the Telfords presented problems, because they could have been warned off him by their daughter.

He brought up that difficulty when Christa phoned to tell him she wouldn't be coming home that weekend. She actually used the word 'home', which softened the disappointment. But the wonderful lift of the heart when he heard her voice did not last for long.

"There's a special *Egypt of Rameses II* exhibition at the British Museum that all the Egyptian History students are going along to on Saturday," she said. "And I'm going to spend quality time with my boyfriend."

The word, as always, sent a dagger to Graham's heart.

"Oh? And which boyfriend is this?"

"Sean. Haven't I told you about him? He's quite nice."

"Are you going to bring Sean to meet me?"

"You're joking, I take it. This is not the nineteenth century. I never took any of my boyfriends home to meet Mum, and

I'm not going to start now. He's *just* a boyfriend. It's not a long-term thing. I am only nineteen, remember."

"I'll remember. And that I'm not your parent. Talking of which —"

"Yes?"

"I'm trying to think of the best way to approach Terry Telford's parents."

"Really?" There was a feeling of ears being pricked up.

"Yes. I don't think I should approach the man himself without having some idea of his background. Was it really a happy childhood? Was he idolised as his sister said? If so, why does he apparently feel so passionately about the man he believes is his natural father? I need to get a lot of background filled in."

"Yes, I can see that," said Christa thoughtfully. "You have their address don't you?"

"And a telephone number. I think maybe they should be rung first, and told what the interest in them is. Apparently they're fine, gentle people —"

"Da – Graham. Are you working up to suggesting that I do the contacting and the talking?"

"Yes. As a matter of fact I am."

"Then will you let me handle it my way? I'm not completely insensitive, or a complete idiot for that matter. I'll have to tell some lies, but I'll make them as few as possible. Mum's put me right off lies, and Adam too. We try to stick to the truth, if not always the whole truth. Now leave me to think up a plan for the approach, and I'll report back as soon as possible."

"Have a nice weekend," said Graham, rather distantly.

She is moving in with her new boyfriend, he said to himself bitterly as he put down the phone. Would this one last any longer than that last one, whose name he had forgotten (and probably Christa had too)? Even though Graham already hated this new boy, Sean, he was acknowledged by Christa to be no more than a temporary expedient. And she had nearly called him Dad! OK, it was almost natural, when she had been taught to think of him as her dad for most of her life. But he didn't like it at all. It made his interest in her seem almost incestuous. He would much rather be called a dirty old – well, middle-aged, and hardly even that – man, than be called Dad by the object of his…But he couldn't finish the sentence with the most obvious word: lust. It was not lust. He knew all about lust. This was a quite new emotion to him, and he wasn't even going to water it down to 'affection'. This was what people called love.

He filled in his time. He made notes for his next novel, and wondered whether he was ever going to write it. He wrote letters to *The Times* which were not printed, though they still sent little form-letters of thank-you, which he thought rather quaint. He did crosswords and had his hair cut. Over the weekend he thought a lot about Christa and Sean (was he Irish? Was he a hot, sexy little sparrow who would leave Christa desolate? No, he rather thought not. If that sort of affair ever happened to Christa it would not be for a few more years yet).

On Saturday afternoon he went to a football match. It was an important game, Adam said, and he was one of the strikers. The change from an urban school to a rural one had done wonders for Adam's prospects as a sportsman. In Romford he had agonised over whether he would make the school's Under-fifteens team. In Suffolk he was not only inevitably a team member: he was its star. Good humour burst out of him every day when he came home from school. Graham blessed the transformation from the boy he had first seen in Luigi's, and thought the least he could do was go along to the match.

For the first quarter of an hour Graham thought he had never endured a more tedious experience in his life, though he cultivated an involved look, and cheered when the parents around him cheered. After the half-time break, with chat to village people he knew, he thought he had got the hang of the game's rules at last, and he decided it might be an improvement on the awful and tedious rugby he had endured at school. By the end he was cheering with a degree of conviction and commitment. Adam scored a goal, and Hepton Magna won three-one.

He was enormously relieved when Christa rang him on Tuesday evening. She had seen the Telfords and talked to them. Typical author, Graham made notes while she told him about it.

Christa had thought long and hard about how best to approach Terry's parents, and in the end she decided it was best to tell them what she really was: a student. The pretence would merely be that she was studying the Social Sciences, with particular reference to children's concerns. The story was that she was writing her final term's special report, which in her case was on adoption.

"I know you have an adopted son, and I have the impression that the adoption has been very successful," she said on the phone to the woman with the gentle, elderly voice. "It's important to me to have several case-histories because it is so easy to concentrate on the adoptions where there have been problems, even disasters, because they usually make such fascinating reading. But the result is an emphasis on negative aspects, so that the report overbalances. In many ways adoption in Britain is a wonderful success story – as it seems to be in your case, with your son."

"Oh, I'm sure you're right. But how did you know about Terry?"

"By a stroke of luck, really. I have a friend at college, an older woman, who has a child in primary school. One of the children in her class is adopted, and some of the other children were making silly comments about this, and your son told the class that he was adopted, that he had had the best childhood it was possible to have, and he would be eternally grateful that he was chosen as a baby by you and your husband."

"That sounds like Terry. He's a lovely boy."

"There are issues of confidentiality here, Mrs Telford, so I ask you not to bring this up with Terry, or talk about the interview at all. If you are willing to talk to me, that is."

"Well...I don't see why not."

"Of course I'd bring proper identification, and a letter from my tutor explaining that I am a bona fide student, and this is a part of my course at the College. That's standard practice. You can't be too careful these days."

"Oh, that's true. Well, I'll be happy to talk to you. I can't answer for Derek, but he's as proud of Terry as I am, and I think he will talk to you. He's been a university teacher himself, so he's very much on the side of students who have course work to do. They don't always get the co-operation they should, and he knows it's an important part of their degrees."

And so it was arranged. Christa got one of the letters she had received when she registered at the Jeremy Bentham College, photocopied the letterhead, then sweated over a letter from a mythical teacher in the Social Studies department. She thought of using some impenetrable jargon in it, and one or two deliberate spelling mistakes, but thought this might be clever-clever rather than clever. Anyway, she hadn't been told what Derek Telford had been a university lecturer in, so she had best be careful. The letter she finally came up with was short, simple and factual (except that it was pure fiction). Christa's joy in composing it proved she was her mother's daughter, whatever she said.

Another part of her preparation was to have in her mind a few examples of other families she had interviewed with examples of practices and experiences that ranged from the catastrophic to the euphoric, and could be quoted during the interview: "to give verisimilitude to an otherwise bald..." but her memory of the quote failed her at that point.

She was on the whole rather pleased with her preparations. In fact, she felt she was on the way to becoming a fiction writer. She glowed with confidence when she rang the bell of 27, Commons View, in Wimbledon, the address which Graham had got from the London Telephone Directory.

"Oh hello, it's Christine Worcester, isn't it? I'm Eve Telford." The woman was in her sixties, dressed in an interesting olive-green woollen dress, with a simple but feminine hairstyle and glasses. "Do come in. You look too young to be doing a thesis."

"It's more like a long essay," said Christa. "But I think I may go on studying after graduation, so it will be a good practice for when I write a thesis. It's the biggest thing I've done in my life, and very exciting!"

"I'm sure it is. I thought we'd talk in here. Do sit down. The kettle's on. I won't be a minute."

The sitting room was neat, simply furnished but comfortable and homely. Newspapers were obviously an important element in the Telfords' lives, being strewn around in sections. Television was much less so, being tucked away in a corner, even looking dusty. Mrs Telford came back with a tray, and handed Christa biscuits and poured her a cup of tea. Christa took out a notebook and prepared to write, or pretend to.

"Is this the house that Terry grew up in?" she asked.

"Yes, it is. It's near enough to the Common to be ideal. And occasionally if we were hard up we could let it out during the tennis and all go to the seaside."

"Was Terry an only child?"

"Oh no. We have a daughter, Sarah – our own – but I couldn't have another child. We longed for another to make the family complete: a son, not because we are dynastic in any way, but just to have – I don't know – experience with both. And our daughter longed for a sibling to play with, but more to cuddle and nurse and boss around a bit. She did all of those things!"

"And the adoption was arranged officially?"

"Oh yes, of course. We could have been in great trouble if it had been done in any other way. They did hand a letter to us, at the request of the mother. We've kept it always. It just said the baby boy was much loved, she would have done anything to keep it, but she was too young, and her parents didn't want the baby to spoil her life. She said he was healthy and determined, like his father, who was in the services, and she hoped he and we would be happy. It was signed 'Peggy', with no surname or address. The local authority people would have insisted on that, at the time."

"I suppose you've kept it ever since?"

"Oh yes – well hidden! We wanted it in case Terry ever became curious about his origins. But luckily he never has."

"Luckily?"

Mrs Telford began to look a little fierce.

"I'm perhaps prejudiced, or at least behind the times. You

read all these stories in the papers about heartwarming reunions, new ties with the birth mother and so on. But there must have been just as many that have turned out disastrously – fresh rejections, or finding out that you've nothing in common. So I think Terry is very wise not to go in for that sort of experiment. Though naturally we feel an enormous gratitude to the birth mother."

"I'm sure…For anything more than giving up her child?"

She screwed up her face.

"Well, though we'd always been told we weren't to try to make the child a carbon copy of ourselves, I think the letter reinforced that very usefully: the father a soldier, the mother writing a rather flowery letter (though she was very young, of course) – those things meant we never expected Terry to be a great brain. Does that sound patronising? I don't mean to be. He'll be a wonderful primary schoolteacher, and the children will love him, but he always had to work hard in school and later. A great heart, not a great brain…Oh, there you are, Derek. Come and sit down, and put your spoke in when you feel like it."

Derek Telford was lean to the point of emaciation, but bursting with energy and enthusiasm. He joined in with his wife in a resumé of Terry's early years, the toys he had loved most, his first words and steps, his first day at school, and so on. They weren't the sort to keep a photo-album of Terry's Great Moments, but they certainly had on tap its verbal equivalent. In the course of the conversation Christa learnt that Derek himself had become, after years as a schoolteacher, a lecturer in aerodynamics at the City University. Terry had been fascinated by any scientific experiment that Derek tried out at home, but his father had discovered that this interest was entirely in the spectacle: the scientific significance had never impinged on him at all.

"It wasn't easy for him later on," said Derek, "deciding what he wanted to do with his life – I mean as far as work was concerned, because that's only part of what you do with your life, isn't it? He was restless, with no particular direction."

"But always coming back here, because it is the centre of his life, and we are all such *friends*," said Eve. "He took a gap year after his Advanced Level exams. His results weren't marvellous, and didn't really point the way for him. He had a good year off from study, working in a hospice, then in a hostel for children at risk. He really grew up in that year. Then he started at the University of North London, mainly courses on Education. He had a tiny bedsit, and came home here at weekends. Easing the process of moving out, he said – though I rather think he meant *for us*."

"He was wise," said Christa. "I should have done that."

"Then Derek got an offer, didn't you, dear?"

"That's right," said Derek, grinning broadly and all but rubbing his hands, his pride quite unconcealed. "It was an article I'd had in the Journal of Aerodynamic Studies, and it made a little bit of a stir, you know – a stir in a tiny circle, inevitably. And the next thing I knew, I got the offer of a year's sabbatical research and teaching at a university in Indiana. Well, I was coming up to retirement here, due for leave, and everyone was very kind, so it was arranged and off we all went."

"When was this?"

"Three years ago, in September."

"And Terry came with you."

"Oh yes. We talked it over, got what the Americans call a catalogue from the university to see what courses were on offer, and there were lots of things that appealed to him. Of course we were all worried a bit about interrupting his courses here, because we didn't know if his American courses would be accepted towards a degree. But in the end we all felt it was too good a chance to miss."

"In what way too good?"

They looked at her as if she was being rather dense.

"Well, what other chance was he likely to get to live abroad, see how other nations live, experience another culture?"

Plenty of chances, Christa thought, ones which he could make himself, and more challenging ones. The United States, after all, was hardly the same as taking off for Ulan Bator or New Guinea.

With the antennae of an independent young woman, Christa was beginning to suss out the Telfords. They were cultivated, liberal, open-minded people who were also clingers to their children. They knew it was what parents should not do, but their intelligence provided them with a great range of reasons that in this or that case they were justified in going against the accepted wisdom. She understood why Terry felt he had to get away. She also understood why, in looking for his natural mother, he had kept his search quiet. His parents, while saying it was very understandable and they were not in the least hurt, would have subliminally let it out that they were.

"It must have been an exciting time for all of you," she said.

"It was," said Derek. "We were on a lovely campus, an hour from Indianapolis, acres of space, and Sarah got in with the local women's groups and charitable organisations. I was hard put to it to tailor my teaching to students who had had an education in some ways very different to ours here, but I coped."

"That must have been difficult for Terry too."

"He coped too, wonderfully. You know the young – well,

you're one of them! You can accustom yourselves to new things much more quickly than us oldies. Terry makes friends easily, so he got a lot of help, and put together with their advice a crash reading course to bring himself up to scratch. They really were a lovely bunch, his friends, and quite soon we were hardly seeing anything of him. In the vacations he took off to travel around a lot more of America and Canada. We didn't try to stop him – it was the best opportunity he was ever going to have. And he rang us every two or three days to tell us he was all right, and what he'd been doing."

And sent his laundry back to be done too, Christa wouldn't have minded betting. There was one thing to be said for a mother who refused to be treated as a washerwoman: it gave a tremendous fillip to the drive for independence.

"So since you came back here Terry's been working as a teacher?" she said.

"That's right. A supply teacher. They're desperate for them. Not that Terry won't be a first-rate teacher – I'm quite sure he will." Eve seemed to be dimly conscious that she wasn't making an altogether favourable impression. "But he's not really qualified yet, and he's doing some course with the Open University. With those, and his American courses recognised, he can qualify and get a permanent job. Outside London, we hope. The schools in London are just too tough for a young teacher. And Derek is retired now, so we can look around for a home in the country. Like most pensioners we fancy a slower pace, a bit more peace and quiet."

You'll get that, thought Christa, if you move to a small town where you don't know anyone. Anyone but Terry.

"And then perhaps grandchildren," she said.

"We'd love that," said Eve, and Derek nodded. "Sarah, that's our daughter, has had lots of relationships, but she's never shown any sign of wanting to settle down with any of the men, let alone having children."

"Terry's had girlfriends," said Derek. "Girls he's really fond of, but not one that's serious enough for him to bring home."

"Of course if he were gay we wouldn't mind in the least – it would make no difference whatsoever to our feelings for him." Eve protested too much, Christa thought. "But to be honest we'd prefer him to have a wife or partner, and children. It would somehow seem *right* – that life goes on, I mean."

Christa kept having to remind herself that she liked the Telfords very much. It must have been wonderfully exciting, having such liberated and lively-minded people as parents. At first. Before too long the emotional blackmail of which they were so obviously unconscious must have got to be a burden, a smothering blanket, something to escape from. Terry must have had hundreds of little escape mechanisms. Otherwise how could such loving parents remain uncertain whether or not he was gay?

Christa said as much to Graham, when she reported back to him on Tuesday. She was as fair to the Telfords as she knew how to be, but that fairness included, perhaps especially included, her half-brother Terry.

"When we saw him and Mum together," she said, when they got on to a general chin-wag, "it was like two children playing together. A bit nauseous. But I think I understand now. They were the sort of people, his parents, who would only buy non-racist, non-militaristic, environmentally-friendly toys for their child. Everything would be talked over at great length at some sort of family meeting, and there would be emotional pressure of the most subtle kind that it would take any child a long time to get a handle on. I can understand why he might want to have a silly, childish time with someone, with no concealed agenda – or apparently none."

"I take your point," said Graham. "Well, I'm going to have to have a talk to Terry. I think it would be best to talk to him openly, with no tricks or subterfuges this time."

"You don't have any choice," said Christa tartly, "since he's already met you."

"What I meant was: be straight that what I'm interested in is Peggy's death, and how she came to meet it. But also, of course, I'm interested in how he came to have another natural father in addition to me. I suppose the answer must be your mother's inveterate tendency to lie, but I want to get at how it came about."

"Well, he's teaching in Peckham this week," said Christa. "That came out when the Telfords and I were making conversation as I was leaving."

"And he teaches in primary schools," said Graham. "It's a start."

The first school he rang on the list in the telephone directory said that Terry Telford had taught there in the past, but was not there that day.

"He's teaching in this school all week," said Graham.

"Ah – that could mean it's a school with real problems," said the voice. "Try Selford Green or Winslow Road."

And it was at Winslow Road that Graham found him, and was given the number of the staff common room and told to ring back in the lunch hour.

"Terry Telford here," said a slightly suspicious voice when Terry had been fetched.

"Terry, this is Graham Broadbent here. You remember me from —"

"Of course I remember you." Brusque, but not unfriendly.

"It seems to me we're in a bit of a mess. You know about

Peggy's death?"

"I've talked to the police about that."

"So have I, and they've been very reasonable. But I think you and I have an interest in what has happened that may not be of a criminal nature."

"What nature then?"

"Of a human kind. To start with, I was told by Peggy – virtually told – that you were my son. I'm not sure I shouted 'whoopee', any more than you shouted 'whoopee' when you were told at the dinner I was your father. But it surely leaves us with something to sort out, which is probably something quite distinct from anything the police are investigating." Silence. "Well, doesn't it?"

"I suppose so…I just feel I have nothing to say to you…But if you feel you want to talk, that's fine by me. I've got a small flat – a glorified box really – on the borders of Peckham and Camberwell. It's 21 Tetleigh Road, flat 6. When would you want to come?"

"Tomorrow night?"

"Tomorrow it is. But remember: I'm not your son."

15

The First Son

Tetleigh Road was a short street of fairly substantial late Victorian houses, and number twenty-one was at the end of the cul-de-sac, and had a panel of eight bells by the blue-painted front door. When Graham had stated his identity to Terry Telford a buzz sounded; he went in and proceeded as directed up the stairs to the second floor, thinking it felt more like living in New York than London (it was, in fact, a long while since Graham had lived in London). The flat, which he was ushered into by Terry, was no more than a flatlet, with kitchenette, bathroomette, and a bed-sitting room with hideaway bed. It was rather ingeniously planned, given the restrictions imposed by its consisting of two of the house's original bedrooms, one very tiny, and Terry had made it pleasantly habitable with large posters of American cities and purveyors of crap music. There were records and books, but Graham always felt embarrassed at looking at the bookshelves of other people because they jumped to the conclusion that he was searching for his own books, or, at the very best, subjecting their tastes to an impromptu critique.

Terry was relaxed and moderately welcoming, but the welcome did not extend to actual friendliness. Graham also felt that he was tensed up. The coffee he was offered was the real thing – a relic of Terry's upbringing, probably – and there was the sort of cake, with currants, cherries and candied peel – that bore witness to a sweet tooth.

"It's a nice pad," said Graham, sipping to mask an awkwardness. "It's much more difficult than it was in my day for young people to get a foothold on the market."

"Much more," said Terry, sitting down opposite him and striving to relax. "Eventually I'll move elsewhere, but I'd like a few years in London on my own before I do that."

"That's another problem with the housing market – young people stay at home longer than they did in my day. I loved my parents, but the moment it was possible I was away and on my own. Nowadays you stay longer, and the longer you stay, the more difficult it becomes to strike out on your own."

"True," said Terry. "But in the end it builds up and it's something you're screaming to do and get it over with."

"Parents clingy?"

Terry shrugged.

"A bit. There are many worse, that I do know. I owe them everything, so I'm loosening the bond gradually. All parents have a bit of that sort of clinginess. All real parents."

Graham felt stung.

"Touché. Can I make one thing clear? My affair with Peggy – much too sweeping a word but it must serve – lasted a few days: four separate occasions, if you want the exact reckoning. After that there was no contact until this year. If you were the result of what we did —"

"I wasn't."

"— then I was never told. What I would have done if I had been (and knowing Peggy now I realize I could have been told even if it wasn't true, so I was really lucky) I don't know. Probably ducked out if I could. I never felt the glow of parenthood, even when I felt sure – stupidly – that you were my son."

"That's lucky then," said Terry, with a wry smile. "Funny, isn't it? The people I know who have the glow of parenthood more than anyone else are the Telfords."

"Yes. I gather they love you very much."

"They do. And I them. I'll always be there if they need me, and they will for me. So why do I sometimes think of that Oscar Wilde line about 'She loved him with a love that made his life a burden'…? I suppose the trouble is that they'll also be there when I don't need them. So it becomes necessary to do things that they know nothing about."

"Girlfriends?"

"Yes. The odd boyfriend too, but that never worked out."

"And finding out who your real parents were?"

"Yes."

Terry put down his cup and thought for a time.

"Don't hurry it," said Graham.

"It was when we were about to go to America," Terry said eventually. "Derek had got a year's professorship in a university in Indiana. I was excited, but a bit in two minds, because it meant I wouldn't 'break the bonds' for another year at least, and I was conscious of time passing. I suddenly felt I wanted to *know*. And that was accentuated by the fact that *America*, as a prospect, had obviously caused them to think a bit, put them in a bit of a quandary. Why, I didn't know, and they certainly weren't telling me. I heard the word over and over, from outside the door. That was perfectly natural, you might think, since the whole trip was an adventure for them too. But what wasn't natural was that they always cut short the conversation when I went into the room."

"You felt it would have been natural to them to share their thoughts with you, since you were going with them?"

"Of course. And my going with them was what they wanted. So what were they keeping from me? What were they afraid of?"

"So you raided the family safe for the letter from your mother?"

"Family safe? Good Lord, the Telfords don't have a family safe. Anything valuable they may have is used, seen. They would think it immoral to lock things away." He suddenly shot Graham a piercing glance. "How did you know about the letter from my mother?"

"They spoke about it to someone I know."

Terry thought.

"You mean you put somebody on to them?"

"Yes. Not a private detective or anything like that. It was Peggy's daughter, whom you met – your half-sister Christa. I'm sorry, but it seemed necessary. She liked them very much. They know nothing about the connection between her and you. I do want to find what was *behind* Peggy's murder – not just the facts, but the impulse that led to it."

Terry remained in thought, then nodded. Graham breathed a sigh of relief.

"They'd told me once they'd had a letter from my mother, but I hadn't been interested then – much to their relief, I imagine. I didn't want to hurt them, so instead of asking to see it I went looking for it. I knew their habits, so it was quite easy. It was in an unmarked envelope at the bottom of one of Eve's underwear drawers. Incredible, isn't it? It must have been there, or somewhere like it, for over twenty years."

"But the letter didn't tell you her name, did it?"

"No. It was signed 'Peggy', but I thought that might be an assumed name. No, what it told me was that my father was an American serviceman."

Graham nearly dropped his cup. He set it down abruptly, then sat looking at Terry, astounded.

"What a bloody fool I am," he said at last. "Why on earth didn't I think of it? Why didn't I ask myself that?"

"Ask yourself what?"

"What Peggy was doing in Upper Melrose."

"Where on earth's that?" asked Terry, frowning.

"Essex. Or maybe just over the border into Suffolk. With a wonderful Anglo-Saxon church. It was where Peggy and I met up a few weeks after the school play we were in, and it all started."

"So? What's the connection?"

"An American air base, only seven miles away. Its name was Calton Heath, I seem to remember. One sometimes saw the servicemen in the pubs around. They were rather popular."

"Ah. I see."

"Peggy told her parents she went there visiting a friend who lived in Lower Melrose. She was a friend of convenience, I suppose. I was in the church, seeing all the things the guidebook said I ought to see, and when I came out there was Peggy. But she had no interest in architecture, still less in gravestones. She must have been there to meet her lover from the American air base, and he hadn't turned up. So she took me instead. I should have had the modesty to ask myself why she looked at me twice."

"But you say you knew her already?"

"Oh yes. Shaw's St Joan. But I only had a tiny part in Scene I, then shouted rhubarb occasionally after that. She was Saint Joan. Of course there was a lot of talk about her, but it was always the sporty boys she was coupled with in the gossip, not the spotty ones...But probably she found all of us horribly inexperienced. Probably she got her kicks elsewhere."

"I think she did. The affair with the airman went on for several months."

"I see...Until her parents took her off to Romford, I suppose."

"I wouldn't know about that. I didn't talk to Ken much

about my mother. I knew by then I could find her if I wanted to."

"Ken?"

"Ken Poldowski. My father."

"I see…I suppose finding out that he was an American just when you were about to go to America was like a gift from the Gods?"

"I don't think like that," said Terry with a dismissive gesture. "But it couldn't have been more convenient. I spent the first months over there getting acquainted with the system, with people, with habits and attitudes that at first seemed strange. Then round about November I put an appeal on the Internet, with my date of birth, a probable location of London or the South-East, and an appeal to American servicemen who were in that area in the late Seventies and who thought they might be or know about my father."

"A fairly wide net," commented Graham. "A lot of the American bases are in the East or the South-East of the country."

"I know, but I didn't know it then. Anyway I thought it was worth a try. This wasn't the crusade of a lifetime, something I'd have given my right arm to succeed in. I was interested, but I wasn't obsessed. The Telfords were and are my real parents, and with all their foibles I could have done much, much worse with natural parents."

"I'm sure you could."

"Anyway, for a long while there was nothing. Or rather, just one or two answers that I thought were a bit iffy…suspect. Middle-aged men who were vague about England, and seemed just interested in getting in touch with younger men. Then at last there was something: an answer from this guy Kenyon Poldowski."

"What marked him off from the others?"

Terry smiled, self-deprecatingly.

"I don't know. He just sounded genuine. He gave details of his war service in Vietnam, his divorce from his first wife, his posting to Britain, the base in Suffolk, with mention of Ipswich and Colchester as places fairly nearby that he went to periodically. And just a simple statement that he had fathered a boy he had never seen while he was stationed there."

"Quite a lot of the servicemen there could have said the same," commented Graham.

"Oh yes, I know that. But sometimes – just sometimes – you have to go on gut instincts. It was coming up to Easter. I was going to travel around to see more of America. I asked whether I could pay him a visit. He gave me the address of a nursing home for ex-servicemen in Wyoming. Said he was recovering from cancer, doing well, and would look forward to seeing me."

"So you went way off the tourist trail on your travels."

"I did. On the way to San Francisco I did a detour, and when I rang my mum and dad later that week I said I'd been in San Francisco for three days, when in fact I'd just arrived. Somehow they're the sort of people you have to get into little deceptions with. Otherwise there are too many questions. Anyway, I went to the home he mentioned, just outside Cheyenne, they showed me through to the sun-room, I saw Ken and he saw me, and somehow – Bingo!"

"You knew?"

"We knew. Both of us."

"How?"

Terry shrugged.

"The cut of the face. Thick eyebrows, the jaw, the build generally. We looked, then Ken laughed and held out his hands, and we hugged and laughed, and it was…lovely."

"You don't think it happened because you both so much wanted it to happen?"

"No, I don't. It was *right* – felt right and was right. I could see that Ken had been ill, really ill, but I could still see what he'd been like as a young man – not just physically, but what sort of guy he was. He was very warm and human, and he was *straight*. In the sense of uncomplicated. It was lovely just sitting there, talking to him, telling him about college in Indiana, what was strange to me, what reminded me of Britain, friends I'd made, what Derek was doing and what Eve said about the women's groups she was joining. Then we went on to life in Wimbledon, growing up, what I wanted to do with my life, even American politics – everything! Mostly we were alone in the room, so we just babbled on, and the more we talked, the more we took to each other."

Graham found him endearing, but he worried too about a vein of naiveté in him, one which he could not bear to preach caution to.

"And that's why, when Peggy announced that I was your father —"

"I felt outraged. Insulted for Ken. I knew he *wanted* to be my father, and I certainly wanted that too. I'd never talked over my father with Peggy the two or three times we had met. If we had she'd have known better than to do what she did. But she hadn't seemed to want to discuss the matter, and I didn't need to."

"I expect she didn't want to because she was preparing this big, theatrical dénouement, all in the public gaze."

Terry's eyebrows rose.

"I hadn't thought of that. But it does sound very like Peggy."

"She had no private, real self. But looking at it the other

way: didn't you talk about her with your father?"

"Not much. At one point, after we'd been discussing what my parents had been doing while they were in America, Ken said, out of the blue, 'I thought Peggy brought you up herself.' That was when I realised she'd put her real name on the letter. So I said no, she'd given me up for adoption, and I was glad she had, because I had wonderful parents. That was true, but I suppose I also said it to assuage my conscience a little."

"You felt you were going against their wishes in seeking out your dad, is that it?"

"Something like that. Though I'm going to have to do that more and more as I start being myself. Being myself and not just their son. Anyway, when I'd told Ken what had happened, all he said was: 'She was such a lovely girl,' and the subject was dropped between us. We had two days of talking and swapping jokes, and him telling me about Vietnam and being in Britain, and his second marriage. His wife had died a couple of years before – cancer too – and he was living with his sister. We even talked religion."

"That's something my generation scarcely ever did," said Graham.

"He's a lapsed Catholic. I should think they often do. We didn't come to any grand conclusions. It was just a wonderful two days, and we knew we'd be wanting to meet up again and do the same some time in the future. He was scheduled to be released from hospital in two or three weeks, and he said when his sister retired he and she would come to Britain. That hasn't happened yet, but we keep in touch: ordinary letters, e-mail, postcards if we're in unusual places. We joke as if we'd known each other all our lives and know exactly what amuses the other, which in fact we *do*. I can't tell you what a revelation it's been. We both see it as a small miracle."

"But when you came back you decided to contact Peggy."

"Yes…I wasn't sure, but I'd had such a good experience with my father. I took my little piece from the website, rewrote a couple of sentences, and put it on the Find Your Family site."

"And you got a letter pointing the finger at Peggy Webster as the likely mother."

"Yes. It's the sort of thing that happens when you put things on the web. A wonderful stroke of luck, but a bit mysterious." A thought seemed to cross his mind, and he threw a quick questioning glance in Graham's direction. Then he shrugged. "Anyway, as I think you know, I got in touch with her, we met, and you'll have seen from the restaurant that we got on pretty well, on a certain level. I told all this to Sergeant Relf, the man from the Romford police."

"Oh yes, you said they'd been in touch."

"That's right. There was someone higher up, but Relf seemed to be the most clued-up. Luckily when I got home that night – the night Peggy disappeared – I went to beg some coffee from a girl in the flat downstairs, and – well, one thing led to another and I was there all night. So I'm pretty much out of the picture."

Out-ish, Graham thought. Testimony from a sleeping partner must be pretty much on a par these days with testimony from a wife. He was willing to bet that Relf still had half an eye at least on Terry, since he was so securely in the centre of the picture.

"I don't really know how you and Peggy got on," he said. "Only what I saw in the restaurant."

"Ye-e-es," said Terry, seeming to be faintly embarrassed. "I suppose you thought I looked more like a gigolo than a long-lost son."

"Not quite that," said Graham. "But there seemed to be quite a lot of play-acting involved."

Terry frowned.

"Even that's not quite it. We thoroughly enjoyed each other's company – had fun, basically. The odd thing was that fun was *all* it was. It was so unlike meeting my real Dad. That was an emotional experience, something I'll remember, that will be part of me, for the whole of my life. But meeting my real mother was – turned out to be – just a few hours when we thoroughly enjoyed each other's company."

"Was this because you were so similar?"

"Possibly…To tell you the truth, I hope not. But we laughed, and she flirted, and I responded, and really it meant very little. Meant nothing, in fact. It never occurred to me that this was a relationship that would last beyond a few meetings. At best it would be a question of cards at Christmas and birthdays. Something to talk about, happily, with my grandchildren."

"But what exactly was it you didn't like about her?"

Terry raised his eyebrows at Graham as if he was being stupid, clearly not liking the thing being put so brutally.

"Nothing. Well, hardly anything. I don't think you're understanding. We got on famously, but there wasn't anything *there* that made me want to have a real relationship with her. Unlike with the Telfords, who have their irritating sides – mostly sides they are quite unconscious of. But they are real people, and if I'd just met them on a train I'd realize they were the sort of people who are worth knowing, and I'd hope that something would develop."

Graham cogitated about this for a few seconds.

"But I think there must have been some reason why things seemed to go so well but really didn't gel. Something about her that made you uneasy about it developing into a deeper relationship."

Terry got up and walked around the little room.

"Lack of sincerity, maybe? I knew perfectly well she would never have approached me of her own accord. Unless I'd been rich or famous, of course. When I approached *her* the whole thing became part of a long, big production number that was her approach to life, particularly her own life, in her own mind at any rate. It was amusing being part of that number for a time, but the only person with any sort of star part in it was her, and always would be."

"It's the actressy thing, is it, that you...that didn't attract you?"

"Oh but it did! In the short term. Just as you can be attracted to a sort of girl that you know you would never consider for a long-term relationship – marriage or whatever."

"You played up and played the game, whatever game it was she was currently engaged in, but it was a sideshow in your life?"

"Exactly. What I am most interested in at the moment is detaching myself just a bit from the Telfords, without hurting them more than I need to. That's a real problem, a real dilemma, and it calls for all sorts of skills that I'm not sure I have. But I will try to do it to the best of my abilities, and it's something real and important in my life. Compared to my relationship with them, that with Peggy was mere candy-floss."

Graham nodded.

"I think I'm beginning to understand now why you were so angry when Peggy promoted me to the position of your natural father."

"I was livid! It was degrading something that was real and warm and nourishing in my life to the sort of sub-showbiz PR charade that she made of her life: 'Congratulations! You've won the Peggy Webster Lottery! Here is your father – Graham meet our dearly beloved long-lost son!' All through our relationship she conveniently ignored the fact that I wasn't long-lost so much as dumped as an inconvenient piece of baggage on her journey through life."

"And I suppose I got my promotion to fatherhood because I've got some little repute as a fiction-writer, and she was determined I should have a more central role in that life-story than just a quickly-discarded lay. I've faced up to that likelihood already. When she first suggested (not exactly *said*) that I'd fathered a child, a boy, I was bewildered and didn't know what to think. Now I'm just grateful that I didn't leap over the moon singing 'Yippee!' It's better this way, especially with you being so happy with your real father."

Graham was watching, surreptitiously, Terry's face, and a quick shadow passed over it, and was smoothed over by force of will. It puzzled him.

"There's nothing else you want to tell me, is there?" he asked. "About your father, for example?"

"No, no. Of course I worry about him sometimes. He's recovered from the cancer, but cancers recur. I would just hate to lose him so soon after I've found him."

"Of course, of course. The last thing I'd want is to come between you. Let's take this as one of – no, as the last of – Peggy's lies. And I seem to have acquired her son and a benevolent general guardianship of her daughter, at least for the moment. So my hands are full, and I'm rather surprised to find that means pleasantly full. Heaven knows how it will turn out, but at least they have someone who cares for them, in all senses of the word. Maybe you and they will want to keep contact. Anyway I'll leave you be and take myself off. I hope we can consider ourselves friends, and I'll leave you my card, just in case something occurs to you that you think I'd be interested to know."

They shook hands, and that was that.

Many thoughts went through Graham's mind as he drove home. The first was that the young man he had just talked to and the young man he had observed at Luigi's seemed to be two different souls. He preferred the man he had just met, but he thought he could account for the disparity. Meeting up with Peggy was a sort of relief after the Telfords, admirable people though they were. Peggy was funny, flirtatious, outrageously egotistical – in fact she was a parody of a drama queen, one reduced to suburban life. Terry could breathe, be himself, come down from a moral high horse – as people sometimes give way to the temptation to be appallingly politically incorrect, just for the hell of straying for a time from the ever-narrowing path of acceptability.

But at heart he was the Telfords' child, and always would be. Nurture had won out over nature – did it always, he wondered?

No, of course it didn't. Life was more mysterious and unpredictable than that. Peggy was surely a product of nurture too, though: the blind spoiling of her by her parents, love creating a monster, as it so often did. And when it came to Peggy's two children, Graham had to hope that they would transcend both their genetic backgrounds and their haphazard bringings-up.

Something was worrying away at the back of his mind: it was the old tragic business of the fatal flaw, and the consequences it could have. He could not rid himself of the feeling that Peggy brought her death on herself, and that it was probably the result of her inability to tell the truth – her preferring an invention to a fact, where it was more entertaining, more flattering to herself and her talents, more likely to bring her profit – any sort of profit: an access of glory or notoriety as much as financial gain.

And there was one piece of the jigsaw that was not yet fitted in – no, not a piece: the last piece always fitted in, if the rest had been put together properly. It was an area that had remained till last the uninvestigated part of the puzzle – a blue sky or a piece of deep shade. He was going to have to empty those pieces from the bag he had stored them in, sort them out as far as was possible, and then make them contribute to the total picture.

He had a sense that he needed to do it quickly.

16

Back in Time

"George?"

"Ye-e-es?" George Long's voice rose skywards in command, as if he were rehearsing a herd of prima-donna camels for *Aida* at the Pyramids.

"Graham Broadbent here."

"Ah! My most famous student!"

"What does that say about the rest?"

"Now, no false modesty, young Broadbent. I did also once have the man who designed the costumes for *The Last Emperor* in my class, but on the whole I think you have the better chance of becoming a household word."

"Like Jiff and Persil, you mean?…George, I'm ringing about —"

"Poor old Peggy. I know. I've been expecting you to. And at Brightlingsea too. Not a place I'd associate with crimes of passion, though you may know better. It brought a tear to my eye, I can tell you. But of course I'd seen nothing of her since her St Joan. I had no idea how she'd turned out."

"No…I think I told you I had a chat with her soon after your last birthday bash."

"You did. Were you…close to her during rehearsals?"

"Not at all. But I did meet up with her later, during that summer."

"Really? Did you —?"

"Mind your own business. Oh well, yes, if you must know. But what I'm ringing about is to see if you know who she was going with during those months of rehearsal."

"I always make it my business *not* to know, old chap. Just

think: if anything had come out, what would old Ulick have done – your revered head, if you remember. He'd probably have given the male sinner the boot from school, refused to allow the female one into school grounds, and suspended all school plays that needed female participation for a space of five years. It doesn't bear thinking about. We'd have been reduced to *Journey's End* and *The Quare Fellow*."

"Can't you remember any of them? I remember a lot of conversation behind hands, sniggering and so on."

"You can be quite sure, Broadbent old lad, that the sniggerers were the ones that got nowhere, and the ones that advanced their cause furthest, if we can put it like that, ignored her within the confines of the Grammar School and its grounds."

"So who were they?"

"Good Lord, you expect me to remember after twenty-five years?"

"Was Garry McCartney an ignorer?"

"Can't imagine so. I vaguely recall that what he thought, he showed, but he didn't think much. He was a thug, and much too crude for a girl of Peggy's sophistication. I wouldn't be surprised if she kept all the Colchester Grammar lechers at bay, partly for sheer devilment, partly for the joy of tormenting them, and partly because she was fully occupied elsewhere."

"Ah! How did you know that?"

"She was the only female part in the play, you remember, but she always came with another High School girl, assigned by the Lady Head of the place whose name has gone out of my head. Ostensibly she was Peggy's wardrobe mistress, but really she was a sort of duenna. She was a girl who exuded respectability, like a sort of Deborah Kerr, and she probably shed it on the beach with the local Burt Lancaster."

"Why do you say that?"

"Whenever I managed to hear what they were saying when they were talking together it seemed to be about American servicemen. But it wasn't my business, I desperately needed Peggy for Joan, and so I made sure I never talked about it on school premises."

Putting down the phone after a few more minutes of reminiscences Graham was pleased that he had been right about George being, once released from bondage, a superb gossip, with all the gossip's powers of card-index recall and barely-concealed relish. He got less out of the next call he made because, where George had gained release from his job, Sergeant Relf was still very much inhibited by the police code, and perhaps by a natural secretiveness that made him want to keep the Peggy Webster murder as 'his' case.

"You must understand that we're still at an early stage," he said, his voice lowered as if the KGB were standing a foot away from him. "All options are still open. I'm sure you understand that we can't talk about the progress of the case with anyone who is at all central to the investigations. I realize this is frustrating."

"Oh, I understand entirely," said Graham. "What puzzles me is how Peggy got – alive or dead – from Romford to Brightlingsea. And of course who she was with."

"We have a sighting in Brightlingsea," said Relf. "She made enquiries about B&B at a house there, if the sighting is reliable. That is *all* I am telling you, and it's not definite. I'll say good morning, sir."

"Are the children free to return to the house and fetch things?" Graham slipped this in before Relf had had time to put down the phone.

"Yes. We're done with the place. They'll have no trouble getting in."

The next day, when Adam had finished school, Graham drove him to Romford and they met up with Christa at Milton Terrace. It was several weeks since Adam had been there, and he became very thoughtful as soon as he set foot in his old home. While the two went through their things and no doubt talked long and hard about their futures, Graham slipped off to Luigi's and talked to the proprietor, who was not called Luigi and did not add a's to the ends of every other word except sometimes when the restaurant was open.

"I talked to the police," he said, "I think as formality only, not any special thing. They talk about other customers that night. I could tell them the names of regulars, and of those who pay with credit cards, which is most of them."

"And the people who were eating at that table over there?" said Graham, pointing to one some way away from the table that had been reserved for Peggy's party.

"The Americans. He pay with American Express. His name was more like Polish name than American. You want me to check?"

"No. I don't need it checked. I'm pretty sure it was Poldowski."

"That's it, sir! You're on to him – is he the one —?"

But Graham shook his head and smiled.

Booking a plane to the States was easy. The most timorous nation on earth had decided it preferred to remain in its own (highly dangerous) country for the time being, and the British had decided that the appeal of Disneyland was palling. Graham arranged for Adam to stay at the home of one of his friends for a few days (there was going to be none of Peggy's slapdash neglect of her children's well-being from now on), and on Friday he flew out from Heathrow.

When, after a long and unpleasant journey to Wyoming via

O'Hare, Graham checked into the hotel in Cheyenne he first had a good night's sleep. He then went down to have a consultation with the helpful girl at the Reception Desk who advised him to telephone the local branch of the FW, the Veterans of Foreign Wars, where he found a sympathetic voice. He explained that he was an old friend of a former Airforceman called Kenyon Poldowski – they'd been friends in England back in the late Seventies, and he was keen to look him up again.

"I couldn't usually give you his home address without asking Mr Poldowski," said the woman. "But I'm afraid the news is bad. He's back in the Everglades Nursing Home. If you call them they could bring you up to date on his condition, and whether he'll be able to see you."

"For the last time," was implied. For the first time, thought Graham. I do need to meet him.

On an impulse he decided to drop by, without using the hospital bureaucracy in advance. He was determined this was not going to be a wasted trip. It was mid-morning. He told the taxi driver to leave him at the gates of Everglades, and he walked through half a mile of rolling lawns and flower beds. Land was cheap in Wyoming, Graham thought.

The reception desk at the Home was not fazed by an unexpected visitor. Old service friends were apparently dropping in all the time, and a refreshingly permissive attitude prevailed. Graham claimed once again to be an old friend from Ken's English years – "I hope he remembers me," he said as a sort of insurance – and his name was sent in. After a somewhat nervous two minutes the word came back that Captain Poldowski would be pleased to see him.

"He's very ill," said the nurse in a low voice. "He knows it, because we don't keep illnesses secret here. You can have as long as Ken feels up to it, and then we'll have to ask you to go."

Kenyon Poldowski was lying in bed in a room to himself, with windows open to a long stretch of lawn on which the sun was shining. His face was gaunt, and Graham could only make out a square chin as something that recalled Terry Telford, and not much else. The hands were long-fingered, but veined and lacking force. The most vital thing about him were his eyes, flashing with spirit and eagerness. He was going under, but not without a fight, and enjoyment of that fight.

"I don't recognise you," he said, holding out his hand. "But then, I didn't expect to."

"I suppose not," said Graham, taking the weak, damp hand.

"I saw you walking across the grounds," said Ken, gesturing towards the window. "Somehow your clothes said 'Englishman', and the slimness, and just the way you walk. Do English people still walk? We don't. We drive. Quite a few of the guys here have English friends from their service days, but I got it right, didn't I? You're the fellow who writes novels."

"You're quite right," said Graham. "I didn't know how to introduce myself. It makes me seem a jerk to say 'We shared Peggy Webster for a week or so a long time ago.'"

"It sure does. Or a 'rotter'. I liked that word. Do the English still use it?"

"Not much. It would date someone who did."

"Well, so far as Britain is concerned, I'm dated. Britain is Essex and Suffolk about nineteen seventy-five to nineteen-eighty. I don't suppose you can imagine what that was like for us, particularly for those of us who'd been in Vietnam."

"Like a sort of rest cure, I imagine."

"Yes. A physical rest cure, but mainly a psychological one. We'd been killing people at an age when we should only have been killing wasps or rabbits. Kill or be killed was the order of the day, and we sure as hell didn't want to be killed at twenty, twenty-one. And we'd kill for our buddies who'd gone that way: 'Here's one for Garry' we'd say as we shot an enemy coming out of the jungle with his hands up. It was a nightmare come true."

"And then you got posted to Calton Heath?"

"Oh, not immediately. I was back in the States for a bit. Got married, then got divorced. That was the usual thing with 'Nam veterans. The wives couldn't stand the nightmares and the suppressed violence. Not their fault...not ours either. I was sent to Suffolk in nineteen seventy-five, and that's where the healing began. It was like another world. There were actually people who liked us there. Oh, there were others who hated us and wanted to get rid of us: anti-nuclear campaigners and plenty of young men who were jealous. 'Overpaid, over-sexed and over here' – we heard all the jokes. But there were others. We were invited to people's homes – genteel little tea-parties. They were church-going people mostly. For some of the black guys it was their first time in a white person's house – can you imagine? Even for us it was a different world...That's how I met Peggy."

"At a tea-party?"

"Yes. At a place called Lower Melrose. Peggy had a friend there, and her parents were strong church people, just like my folks, only mine were Catholic. Peggy's friend was helping her with her costumes in some school play, which I heard plenty about in the next few months. This friend had a great act – all starch on the outside, which soothed any fears the parents might have had. But boy! – did she have a reputation with the men at the base."

"So Peggy was around at the tea-party?"

"Yes – just happened to be there – I *don't* think. Demure as they come, asking all sorts of questions about our planes, life in the States, when our leave periods were...When she said goodbye she said 'The Church at Upper Melrose is very interesting, and the churchyard too.' I just whispered 'Thursday at eight.'"

"Simple."

"Oh, very simple." He sighed, and suddenly looked very ill. "And sordid most people would think. Here's the grizzled old veteran, thirty years old, making a date for sex with a schoolgirl. Not nice, not gentlemanly, not British...And yet, that wasn't really how things turned out."

"You fell in love with her?"

"Something like that. Or with the *idea* of her. Does that make sense? You're the literary guy." Graham nodded. "I think now that I hardly began to know the real her. But then: here was this young girl – sweet, passionate, grateful, just happy to be with me, to give me what I wanted, demanding nothing more. Not one of the good-time girls, as the locals called them, who made themselves available to the guys at the base in return for expensive meals, night clubs, good clothes, luxuries of any kind. She was so happy to see me, and so uncomplaining if I couldn't get away when I had promised to meet her."

"She had reason to complain, on one of those occasions at least. She had to make do with me in your place."

"Is that so?" Ken Poldowski's eyes narrowed. "Well, I'm not jealous, and I wouldn't have been jealous then. I knew I wasn't the only one. Why would I be? She was young, I wasn't. I could only give her a tiny bit of my time. But she made clear – she *said* – that I was the main one. And that was fine by me."

"And now and again you managed to get a night or two

away together," guessed Graham.

"*Once*. Once we managed to go away together for a weekend. Peggy told her parents she was going with her friend Katy and her parents to London, to attend some sort of concert and a play. They swallowed it, and we went to a little town in Essex…That was a memorable weekend."

"Why?"

"All sorts of reasons. But one thing that has stayed with me all my life was Peggy's talent as an actress. She *was* a twenty-five year old woman for that weekend – looks, behaviour, clothes (I'd bought them, but she selected them). Only once she let her guard fall."

"Why was that?"

"It was a silly little thing. We were having dinner on the second evening in the guest house we were staying at, and it was fish, and Peggy didn't know how to use the fish knife, and she just picked it up, looked at it in a puzzled sort of way, and then giggled like a schoolgirl. Could have been American, Canadian, French – whatever – but it was totally girlish. And the landlady looked at her, and I think she was glad when we left the next morning."

"Did that sort of thing worry you?"

"A little. Things could have turned out badly for me if she'd gone to the police."

"Why? She wasn't under age."

"Still, if the police had gone to her parents…But anyway, it didn't happen. And we had the most wonderful months together – together only now and then, but still the whole time was idyllic. Of course she was young for me. Sometimes I'd laugh at her. She'd tell me that her mother was a distant cousin of the Duke of Devonshire, but since I had no idea who the guy was, or whether a Duke was a 'sir' or something else, she didn't impress me much. Once the play took over in her mind it was her father who was related to Dame Edith Evans. That had about the same effect. But her youngness and her flights of fancy were part of her charm, and I just smiled at the lies, then."

"How did it all end?"

"Very suddenly. She missed one of our dates in Upper Melrose. That had happened during the rehearsal period for the play, but never since. Then I got a scrawled note, mailed in Lower Melrose where her friend Katy lived. It read something like: 'Things very difficult. I think we're going to move. Parents going through the roof. Will write when I can. I think I am pregnant. All my love, Peggy.' It was the sort of letter a girl might write when she just wanted the affair ended without all the recriminations. But I never really believed it was that."

Graham nodded. Ken seemed to him the sort of man who felt things intensely, a man of emotions, even if his airforce training had made him adept at covering them up.

"But at least when Terry Telford appeared you already had an idea that you had a child in Britain."

"Oh, I had that all right. I want to keep Terry out of this, Mr Broadbent. It's nothing to do with him. But yeah, we'd had a bit of exchange, via e-mail and so on, but when he walked into the room here I said to myself – 'That's my son. He's mine.' Just the chin, I think, but the age too…I've got two kids by my second marriage, a boy and a girl. The boy is twenty-one, and at college, and he's into baseball and computers and rock music. He's a real all-American guy. I saw this young Englishman and I could see that he was naive, puppyish, a bit soft, but you know I was proud to have fathered him. Everyone's idea of a nice young Brit – like your Prime Minister Whatsisname. So we got on really well, and I thought: 'What a great outcome of that weekend in Brightlingsea, or one of those evenings in the churchyard at Upper Melrose.'"

"By the grave of Jonas Braithwaite and his wife Mary Ann," said Graham.

"Now you *are* sounding like a jerk. No, it wasn't nice of Peggy to choose the same grave for her times with you, but then, it was the most private place. And of course I know all about Peggy by now. I've lost all romantic illusions."

"When did you decide to go back to England?"

Ken shot him a quick, shrewd glance. He knew everything had to come out.

"Oh, I'd wanted to for a long time. Since I knew, first time round, that I'd got cancer. Things just got in the way, as you can imagine they do at that time. But since my wife died and my children have been in college and independent I've lived with my sister. Anya was very anxious to make the trip, and we were beginning to get it all mapped out for when she retired."

"And is that what happened?"

"No. She came with me because she had two weeks' vacation coming to her."

"But something else decided you?"

"Yes. I think you're probably guessing what it was. I'd been in touch with Terry on and off ever since he came here. It's been a pleasure, talking and e-mailing and so on. He called me and told me he'd met up with his mother. That was what tipped the balance."

"But you just said you'd grown out of romantic illusions."

"This was no romantic illusion."

His voice was grimmer than it had been so far.

"Then why should you want to see her after all this time?"

"Shall we stick to what happened, and leave why it

happened to a bit later?"

"It's you who calls the shots. But are you strong enough for a long talk."

"Yeah, I'm strong enough. So as soon as I knew that Terry and Peggy had met I booked a flight out and a hotel in London. Before we left Terry rang again and told us about Peggy's dinner that was coming up in the restaurant in Romford, the celebratory meal, and I asked him to book two rooms in a Romford hotel for that night."

"You were going to be there at Luigi's, and Terry knew that?"

"No reason why he shouldn't."

"I don't remember him showing any signs of knowing any people in the restaurant."

"He wasn't meant to. I told him – and it was true – that I wanted to keep all my options open. Notably whether I was going to approach Peggy while I was over in Britain, and if so how that approach was going to be made. I had my back to the Webster table for obvious reasons – my sister Anya faced all of you, and took some digital photos when things grew explosive. You know, I think by the end Terry may even have forgotten I was there. I may be wrong, but somehow when he cried out that he already knew his natural father and it wasn't you, Graham, it was as if he'd forgotten I was there and listening, but he felt for me."

"Stranger things have happened."

"So there I was the whole damned evening, not seeing anything except some shapes and colours in the glass of a picture on the wall of sunny Naples, though I did get a better view of Peggy briefly, when I went to the men's room. That made it easier later on. I got Anya to take those photos – when Terry was making his protest. It was a digital camera, so I had them at once. By then I was paying my bill, and a few minutes later Peggy sailed out of the door. I thought she must be going after Terry or after her other son, the young boy. I took Anya back to our hotel in a taxi. She knew I'd decided to look for Peggy and she perfectly understood. She knew we had unfinished business. After I'd dropped her I went straight to the hotel parking lot and took out the rental car we'd been using during the trip. So I drove around the streets of Romford, pretty aimlessly, just looking to see if I came across Peggy."

"There were quite a lot of people doing that on the night."

"Were there? Well, I suppose I got there first. Peggy was out of luck. She was wearing a full green coat, remember."

"Yes. Rather splendid – and beyond her income I'd have thought."

"Hmmm. She was in a sort of square, nice and open, but not ideal for my purpose. I waited till she went into a darker street, then drove up beside her, put the window down, and said 'Ma'am.'"

"Was she frightened?"

A tiny smile, almost of admiration, played on his face.

"Not a bit of it. Peggy always had nerves of steel. But she didn't recognise the voice or the word: I often used to say it to amuse her – she could never get over being called a 'ma'am'. She just kept walking at the same pace, saying with her stage voice 'If you go on pestering me I shall call the police on my mobile.' I kept up with her and said 'Peggy'. She looked round sharply. I said 'Don't you remember me, Peggy?' She said, a bit wavering, 'I don't know.' I said 'It was back in the Essex days.'"

"That must have narrowed the field."

"Now you're being unkind again. What happened to English gentlemanliness?"

"It never came within a mile of me. Romford is still in Essex. And even in the old days you weren't the only one that Peggy went with."

"I told you, that didn't bother me at all. That wasn't what I had against Peggy. Anyway she looked at me, and after a moment or two she said 'Ken?' like she wasn't quite sure, but almost hoped it was me. And I said 'It's been a long time.'"

"So she was 'almost hopeful', you say. Not afraid?"

"Why do you say afraid?"

"Because of what happened."

"I don't think she was afraid in any way. She said 'How come you're in Romford? Were you looking for me?' and I said: 'We've got a lot of catching up to do. Why don't you jump in?' And she got into the car, and I kissed her and said: 'It's been a long time.'"

"'I kissed thee 'ere I killed thee?'"

"Is that poetry?...The killing came later, and I wasn't intending it then. In fact I found her so adorable, there in the flesh, that I almost forgot...what it was that was biting me. It was like being back in my young days – fairly young: Vietnam took my real young days from me. I kissed her again, a real kiss, not a peck. I repeated 'We've got some filling in to do,' and she said 'I can explain.' But I said 'I don't want you to explain. The filling-in is the lovemaking that stopped suddenly back in nineteen-eighty.' And do you know, I almost think I meant it."

Graham had to hide his impatience to know the whole story.

"Don't hold back on me. To make sense of all this I need to know what was biting you."

Ken shifted uneasily in his bed.

"It will sound so goddam trivial. It wasn't the cause of...the killing, only one of the things that…Oh well. I can't explain myself. I'm not one of those guys who spend their time going deeper and deeper into themselves. Let's just stick to facts. Go back to the time two years ago when Terry came here to see me. We talked about him, what he'd done in Britain, how he liked the States, how he was settling in, how his mum and dad were settling in. Then he said: 'It was easier for Derek, because he's got his work, but I think Eve's found time hanging heavy during the day.'" Ken shot a look at Graham. "You learn self-control in the military, if you're wise. You don't let your face or your body give away every passing emotion. I needed all the self-control I could gather, and I'm proud that Terry didn't seem to notice a thing."

"But why?"

"Because I'd assumed when he talked about his mum he meant Peggy. She'd told me she was bringing him up herself. She told me that her parents wanted her to have the baby adopted, but she insisted she was going to keep him. They forced her to move out, and that was why she needed money. She didn't want to make a formal application or complaint to the airforce authorities, but she thought it right I should pay maintenance. I thought it right myself. The worst I thought she might have done was marry someone called 'Telford' without telling me."

Graham let out a laugh in which there was no amusement.

"My God! Peggy surpassed herself! What she peddled to you was the exact opposite of the truth. So you mean you paid her maintenance all the years that Terry was growing up?"

"Eighteen years. The authorities took it out of my pay-cheque. They were used to that sort of informal agreement, particularly for servicemen abroad who had wives and families back home. They upped the amount depending on inflation.

Sometimes Peggy would tell me of a special need – exchange student visit to France, his own computer – and I'd think about it and usually send her something extra."

"So you were in contact all those years?"

"That's right. Every year on his birthday she'd send me a letter thanking me for his present – usually another cheque – and telling me how Terry was doing, his first step, his first word, potty training – the whole caboodle. I paid up willingly, got warm feelings about the boy and my own generosity. She sent me photos – God knows who they were of. What an idiot! I paid up year after year until he was eighteen. Peggy wrote asking me to pay the tuition for him to go to Oxford, but I knew, or thought I knew, that in Britain you get scholarships to go to the university. Anyway, I think kids should grow up and be independent. So I wrote and said 'No way'. That was the last communication we had until the meeting in the streets of Romford."

"Recrimination time."

Ken looked at him as if still bemused, and shook his head.

"Funnily enough it wasn't. You might think it would be, and maybe I intended it to be, but it wasn't. She knew I'd been reunited (if that's the word) with Terry, and she must have assumed that I knew, but when she muttered 'I've made mistakes' I didn't say: 'Boy – you're right about that.' I just said 'We all have.' And before we'd been driving round Romford for five minutes I said: 'We need to forget the past – all except the really good past. What's to stop you coming away with me, back to our old haunts in Essex?' And she looked at me with an ecstatic smile and said 'Nothing.'"

Graham raised his eyebrows.

"Was it really ecstatic, or a theatrical ecstatic smile?"

Ken shrugged.

"I think it was real, as real as she could be, but it came from all the romantic nonsense she felt about herself: an old love returns, still desperately in love, the old fire is rekindled – all that sort of claptrap."

"Was it all claptrap? Wasn't there a tiny atom of truth in it?"

"There was more than an atom. A widower who's had a good marriage is a lonely guy, ready to be set up. Half of me wanted – well, you can guess. I don't need to strip my soul for you – you write novels I'm told. We all have that romantic self-deception. But her mistake was to think that I could be fooled *twice*. In the military you feel emotional about your buddies and even the guys who are not that close to you. Their lives depend on you and your life depends on them. They can let you down once, but they can't let you down twice. Eventually I was going to wake up to her. But at the time I wondered…I want you to believe I had no thought of doing what I did at that point."

"But you went to Milton Terrace?"

"Is that what it's called? Yes, to pick up 'some things' for a few nights. She told me to wait in the car, and I couldn't work out why."

"Probably she didn't want to be interrupted by her children, and have to deal with them with you there."

"She sure was quick! She said she'd left a note for them, that they'd be all right, because their grandad lived in the town. Then we took off for Essex, the real Essex I remembered, her directing first, then me getting my bearings and my memory back. We seemed to be there in no time."

"What did you talk about?"

"My loneliness. Her loneliness. I think hers was just a consequence of mine. She wanted to match it, then come up with a solution for both of us. Quite soon it moved from being a question of 'if only we'd' to being one of 'we still could'. Nothing crude, you understand, or pushy on her part. It was all done delicately, as if she had a dream, and it was still possible that…"

"Peggy lived in a dream world," said Graham. "I think she always did, but it had grown on her over the years, particularly when it became clear that life wasn't going to live up to her expectations."

"Whose life does?"

"Did she ask you about your children, your financial position?"

"Just a question now and again, but she got the information. And it was true: moderately well off, moderately promising children, me jogging along fairly happily with my sister."

"But you could have been so much happier with her."

"That idea was in the air. Anyway, we got to the Colchester area, and almost simultaneously we said 'Brightlingsea.' Because it was getting to be 'going back time'. Anyway we drove there and went to a few places that said Bed & Breakfast in the window, but most of them had signs that said they were full. It was late, getting towards midnight, and I think they really meant they didn't take people who arrived at that time of night. Peggy said: 'Down by the river, where there used to be all those little boats.' We'd used those derelict little boats before. It was a crazy idea, but it was a clear night and there was moonlight. We left the car on Hurst Green and walked down to the path and the mudflats."

"What was the atmosphere? Romantic?"

"Yes. I was in the silliest of Seventh Heavens. Peggy had apparently put practical thoughts about my financial situation and her two children out of her mind. Even she saw there was an atmosphere that shouldn't be spoilt. We went over the mud to a hulk, and as soon as we got there she was at it – we were…we both were, eager, hungry, but she was, like, greedy. Not greedy for sex, but like it was food and she couldn't get enough. Before long it stopped being wonderful and it almost became…disgusting."

"Like it had never been with Peggy back in the old days."

"No no. Never like that. And when we lay back, she began."

"Began what?"

"Talking on and on. Wasn't that the best sex I'd had in years? Wasn't it? Forcing me to say yes. When we were together it would be like that all the time. We *could* take up again where we left off. Nobody she'd ever known had satisfied her as I did. I could move over here. That wouldn't be a problem. I could move in with her. Was the exchange rate good these days? She hadn't followed it since…She pulled herself up there. She'd nearly said 'since the maintenance payments stopped'. I said the exchange rate was very poor. 'Well, doesn't that mean it would be very good going the other way? I could come to the States and see how I liked it. There are drama groups there I imagine. I have to have my drama – it's my lifeblood. I should think they'd like an English accent for when they put on classic English plays. Are there any good houses we could rent in Cheyenne? I'm not used to luxury but I am used to comforts, and those I do expect. Or do you think I'd be happier somewhere closer to where the action is? San Francisco maybe, or Los Angeles?'"

"I and me and mine were very common words in her conversation," said Graham.

"I saw she was taking me for a fool. Again. For the second time she would screw me for everything she could get. She'd done it for eighteen years, now she'd start all over. I hate being taken for a fool, yet here she was setting me up as a fall guy again. I saw red, but I still had enough control to want her to know what was happening to her. She still had the yellow scarf she'd been wearing with the green coat, and it was on the planks we'd been making love on. I took it, put it around her shoulders as if to keep her warm. Then I began tightening it. 'These are your last moments, Peggy,' I said, and she giggled, thinking it was a joke. 'You bled me dry because you thought I was a fool, but I'm not dumb enough to let it happen for a second time. To me you're a waste of space on this earth –' The face was going scarlet, the eyes bulging, she was trying to pull the scarf away with her hands, but I kept tightening and tightening until…There she was, dead. And I meant what I said. I couldn't see the point of such a self-obsessed, lying, scheming, cheating soul as hers. I was her executioner."

"Self appointed."

He turned wearily towards the window, and the long lawns outside.

"Of course. I'm not justifying myself, or what I did. It was unforgivable. Maybe I'm about to find that out. I'm just trying to tell you what my thoughts were at the time. And if you want to be merciful, perhaps you could wonder whether killing as many as I did in Vietnam doesn't put a person into a different relationship to murder, compared to a civilian who has led a careful, respectable, humdrum life."

Graham was quiet. Who was he to make moral pronouncements? He who had led a conspicuously careful, respectable, humdrum life until now?

"What did you do next?"

Ken lay there, finding it difficult to refocus his mind on the time after the murder. Strength was visibly something that had to be struggled for, attained with relief.

"Got back to the car," he said at last. "The darkness was just beginning to lift. I drove back to Romford, and had a late breakfast with Anya. She asked about Peggy and I just said: 'You don't want to know.' It was open to her to believe we'd had a meeting that was unsatisfactory or acrimonious. I don't think she did, but she knew better than to ask. We had another day or two in London, then took the train to Edinburgh for another few days. Then we got the plane home. I think I behaved normally during that time – cool, taking in all the sights, enjoying myself. I bought English newspapers, but saw nothing about Peggy. Anya may have wondered why I bought British papers, but she didn't ask questions. Like my wife – my second wife – she knows there were things in my past life that make me unlike other people. She had a whale of a time in Britain. After she got back here she was just hoping to return for a longer stay that would include Poland. I guess she'll have to go alone."

He pointed vaguely to his body. It was as if the cancer was not in any one place but in the whole body.

"I think that's really all I came for," said Graham, getting up. "Can I give your love to Terry?"

"You sure can. He telephones now and then, and I talk to him if I'm up to it. He must have guessed by now that there's no hope."

Graham nodded, trying to keep the subject unemotional.

"How long have you got?"

"Oh, the docs don't want to be too specific. Afraid they might be proved wrong. But from the way they're talking it seems like a matter of weeks rather than months."

"I hope it's as easy as it can be."

"It won't be. But that way I'll be glad when it's over. You can tell the police over there that extradition would take a whole lot longer than my judge is going to take to get hold of me."

"I'll tell them. If what you've told me tallies with what they've found out so far, I can't see them going to the trouble and expense of applying for extradition."

"You don't have the death sentence any longer in Britain, do you?"

"No. Not for a long time."

"Just a long, long prison sentence? Seems to me our way is the more merciful way."

"Seems to us that you have managed to have both."

Ken smiled a wry smile.

"Point taken. Keep in touch with Terry, won't you. And you'll be in touch with the other children as well. Peggy may not have been much of a mother, but I feel kinda…"

His voice faded.

"Oh, I'm very much in touch with them," said Graham.

"Don't try to explain it to them. It will sound like I'm trying to excuse myself. Just say it goes back a long way."

"Everything does," said Graham. "Right back to conception. I'll say goodbye. You must be very tired."

He took the hand that could hardly tighten itself round his, then left the sun-soaked room, thanked the woman at Reception and ordered a taxi.

Going out into the sunlight Graham walked down the rolling hill towards the gate, where he had asked the taxi to wait for him. The lawns sloping downwards to the road seemed to image life in its later stages. He got into the taxi, directed it to go to the hotel and then the airport, and began his journey home.

Two weeks later he heard from Ken Poldowski's sister that he had died. Two weeks after that he received from her a photograph, with a note to say that Ken wanted it given to his son, but thought that Graham should see it first. It showed

Ken in American airforce uniform, posing with Peggy, perhaps for her friend Katy. Peggy was wearing a pretty, frilly frock and looked adorable. The picture was taken just outside the lych-gate of the Upper Melrose church. The stumpy tower of the church could be seen to the left of the picture, and in the distance, well into the churchyard, Graham was pretty sure he could make out the tomb of Jonas Braithwaite. He decided not to mention the tomb and its significance to Terry.

17

Family

Once he had arrived back home, Graham's instinct was to bunker down. The record had been set right, the picture had become clear, unclouded at last by Peggy's congenital and virtuostic lying, and the episode could be put behind him as an uncharacteristic blip in a well-ordered and frankly rather dull life.

Except that the 'episode' – too trivial a word, really – was not over, and could not be put behind him. Adam's presence in his cottage was sufficient witness to that, as well as the presence of Christa and Terry further into the background, and still further back the figures of Ted Somers and Harry Webster, who as Adam's grandfather and father seemed likely play a part, whether they wanted to or not, in his life.

So his life, whatever happened, had been rearranged. It seemed perverse or ungrateful to think of his new responsibilities as duty. He was, like it or not, something close to being a paterfamilias. And as soon as he thought of himself in those terms an ache came into his heart. That was not the relationship he had wanted to have with Christa. Now, after the draining experiences of the last couple of months, she represented a new life, vitality, warmth – even fun, a concept he had rarely considered to be a desirable or possible component of existence. And not just fun – love too. Love most of all. He had no doubt that he was in love. Had he ever been in that state before? Even at eighteen, with Peggy? (He did not bother to bring his wife into his calculations.) No, his feelings for Peggy had been merely an adolescent crush, without the same warmth and light that Christa carried with her into his nearly-middle-aged lifestyle.

Graham had a fiction-writer's ability to see character and predicaments from all possible angles. When he got to this point in his analysis he said to himself: no, you have not been in love before. But you have thought yourself to be in love. Believed you were. Quite often. Is this the same thing? Is this one more piece of self-deception?

He rang Sergeant Relf when he had been home two days.

"I think you know the line I was working on," he said, "or guessed at it. I went and talked to Terry Telford's father in Wyoming. His name is Kenyon or Ken Poldowski, and he was the American in Luigi's on the night of Peggy's death. He'd been paying for Terry's upkeep for eighteen years, but of course she'd given him up for adoption —"

"Or simply given him to the Telfords," said Relf.

"Yes. Everyone's very insistent it was all done legally, but Peggy was an actress, and I suspect she fooled her parents. But either way Ken had been fooled. I accept Ken's assertion that this was just a part of what made him kill her, because I found him to be an honest person – one of the straightest I've ever met. He went looking for her that night, and then he found that some of the old magic was immediately rekindled. But before long Peggy threw off the veil of romance and started getting blatant. He realized he was being fooled again. He had a sense too that she was simulating a sexual appetite which was really nothing but an old, straightforward greed for money, security – things she'd always gone after, though mainly as secondary goals to the ones represented by her self-deceptions and her acting. A whole mess of emotions coagulated into a strong revulsion against her and all she stood for in his life, and he strangled her in that old boat at Brightlingsea."

"He told you this himself?"

"Yes. No point in concealing it. He has cancer, a recurrent cancer, and he has only weeks to live. You could contact the Everglades Nursing Home in Cheyenne. His doctors will tell you. He's a fighter, but he's going to lose this one. Going by his looks 'weeks to live' seems about right."

When he put the phone down Graham was struck by a thought that had probably been lurking in the back of his head since Cheyenne: a square jaw was pretty poor proof of paternity. His meeting with Peggy in the Upper Melrose churchyard had been after A-levels, when everyone who was about to leave school simply drifted away because there was nothing left in school for them to do. July – some time in July. And Terry was born mid-April, he had said on the website. Possible, certainly possible. It might be worth going into blood groups...

He put the thought from him as soon as it had occurred. He'd made the point to Christa and Relf, and it remained true: if Peggy had had his child he had known nothing about it at the time, nor for a quarter of a century afterwards. A mother who has borne a child might well feel something for it for the rest of her life, even if she had had it adopted. But a father, one who has been unaware of the birth? How can he suddenly feel something for that child?

And the truth was that he felt nothing special for Terry Telford, beyond a vague hope that he sorted things out with his parents without too much pain for them or him, and got a job that satisfied him. He felt more for Adam and Christa, though he was quite aware that his feelings for Christa were not of a fatherly kind. He had often, in recent weeks, found her in his mind as he drowsed out of sleep. She had become, for him, one of those distant, longed-for, impossible dreams, like a love-goddess to an adolescent.

Added to which, he knew that Terry had felt immediate affection and affinity for Ken Poldowski, and though he suspected the soon-to-be dead officer had not felt emotion of quite the same intensity in return, still he did not want to disturb the boy's orientation of his affections one more time. Let be, let be.

One Saturday, when he had delivered Adam to his grandmother in Stanway, he drove into Colchester and took refuge from the crowds of early Christmas shoppers in Castle Park. It was when he had been round the castle – the first time for twenty-five years – that, standing at the top of the hill, he saw Garry McCartney toiling up it with what looked like three grandchildren running riot around him. Graham resisted the impulse to hurry away, and awaited him by the path.

"Hello, Garry."

The big man blinked.

"Why it's…novelist chappie, isn't it."

"Graham Broadbent. I suppose you read about Peggy."

The face collapsed a little.

"God yes. That took me back. She was such a…star. And they've never nailed the devil who —"

"It was an American. He's died of cancer. He was having it off with her all the time she was playing St Joan. She had his child, then stung him for maintenance even though she'd given the baby to another family for adoption."

The man gaped.

"You can't be —"

"Oh but I am serious. Some of our old memories get just too much of a rosy tinge to them. See you around."

And he walked off. When he looked back Garry was enforcing what passed for his authority with some heavy cuffs around the ears. The children screamed blue murder, but it didn't sound entirely serious.

The next weekend Christa came down, brightening Graham's life, and even causing Adam to come back earlier from his mate's home on the two nights that she stayed. Graham and Christa discovered a mutual fondness for chess, largely fallow for lack of partners, and they played at the dining table while Adam watched a blood-and-technology video from the sofa. While Graham was meditating a move of Christa's whose short-term significance he could see but whose long-term aim was mysterious to him, Christa said (perhaps to distract him):

"I think Grandad and Kath's marriage is several steps closer."

The deafening sound of steel and bass-drums from the TV set was extinguished.

"So does that mean I have to go and live with them?" Adam asked.

"No, it doesn't," said Graham. "You stay here as long as you want it to be your home...But he is your grandfather, remember. He's all you've got left of your mother's family. You could perhaps go and stay with them for some weekends."

"I s'pose," said Adam, starting up the video again. "If there's no match on."

"I'm glad you're still seeing your grandfather," said Graham, turning back to Christa and the game. He moved, and then wished he hadn't been distracted.

"Yeah, I went with Sam."

"Sam?"

"The current."

"A male Sam, I take it," said Graham, to say something, "not a Samantha."

"Of course not. I knew him at school, but I never realised

how nice he was. He protects me from Romford."

"Do you need protection from Romford?"

"Yeah, from Romford people. People who come up and say they remember Mum from *Hello, Dolly* or *Hedda Gabler*, and God knows what. I sometimes think people like that were closer to Peggy than I was."

"I should think actors' children always think that."

Christa threw up her hands.

"She was only an amateur, for God's sake. Not that that creep Michael Halliburton would admit that."

"Why's he become a creep?"

"He always has been. But he offered me the other female part in *Who's Afraid of Virginia Woolf?*"

"What's creepish about that? You're a bit young, though."

"Apart from the fact that he knows I've got *no* interest in acting, what's creepish about it is he said he'd always had a *special* interest in me."

"Oh."

"Which must either have meant that he'd always wanted to bed me, which since Sam was standing beside is unlikely, or he was trying to tell me he was my father. As if I cared."

"I'm sure that's the best attitude."

"Sam told him that having Peggy for a mother put me off the stage for life. He protects me, you see."

"You really like him?"

Christa made an attacking move and her face assumed an ecstatic look.

"I *do*. I really do! He's sweet and gentle and cooks better than I do. I think I'll be moving in before long. His flat is nice too."

"I hope he's good at cleaning and ironing as well."

"He is, actually, but I'd do my share, so stop being so sarky."

"I just don't want you to make a wrong choice, after the shock of your mother's death."

Christa made a move that revealed, too late for Graham, the deadly plan behind her recent manoeuverings.

"I'm not making a *choice*. But he is lovely, and I think I'm beginning to…Oh well, no point in making plans that probably won't work out. But Graham – don't go on about Mum's death being a shock. She never figured much in our lives, and everything that's happened since has been much, much better."

Graham made a move he suspected was his last.

"She's right," said Adam from the sofa.

"Well, I'm glad about that."

"It's good to have someone who *cares* about me," said Christa. "You know, what I said in that hotel in Colchester has come true. I've got a father at last."

"Thanks," said Graham bleakly, folding the board and putting the pieces carefully away in their box.